ONE HUNDRED HUMBUGS

AN ASPEN COVE SMALL TOWN ROMANCE

KELLY COLLINS

BOOK NOOK PRESS

A NOTE FROM THE AUTHOR

I thought I had wrapped everything up with a big ol' bow in *One Hundred Merry Memories*. Really, I did. I even stood back, hands on hips, admiring what I thought was the perfect, heartwarming conclusion to Aspen Cove. But apparently ... you all weren't quite ready to say goodbye.

Message after message (and maybe a few strongly worded emails) came in, asking for more—more stories, more laughs, more love, and more of the charming chaos only Aspen Cove can provide. It turns out this small town had one last tale hidden beneath the snow.

So here we are, back for another round of holiday hijinks in *One Hundred Humbugs*. Because, let's face it, Aspen Cove never really lets you leave. And truth be told, I couldn't resist diving into the fun one more time.

Pull up a chair, grab a cup of cocoa, and let's dive back in!

Kelly

CHAPTER ONE

The alarm clock's shrill buzz pierced through Ruby Whitaker's fitful sleep like an ice pick to the brain. She groaned, blindly slapping at the offending device until it fell silent. The sudden quiet revealed the muffled sounds of the city awakening outside her window—car horns, distant sirens, the rumble of garbage trucks. Another day in paradise.

8:15 a.m. glared at her in angry red digits. Late. Again.

"Shit," Ruby muttered, bolting upright. The familiar knot of anxiety tightened in her chest as she took in her surroundings. Empty coffee cups formed an abstract art installation on her desk, their stained rings a testament to too many late nights spent hunched over her laptop. The acrid smell of old coffee mingled with the musty scent of laundry that needed doing weeks ago.

This wasn't the glamorous freelance life Ruby had envisioned when she'd quit her soul-sucking corporate job two years ago. Freedom and flexibility had sounded great in theory, but it meant never-ending deadlines, clients who expected miracles on shoestring budgets, and a constant, gnawing fear that she was one missed payment away from financial ruin.

She scrambled out of bed, wincing as her bare feet hit the cold hardwood floor. A glance at her phone revealed five new emails, all marked urgent. Ruby's stomach churned. She'd need at least three cups of coffee before she could face that circle of hell.

As she rushed through a semblance of a morning routine—dry shampoo instead of a shower, yesterday's wrinkled shirt smoothed with desperate hands—Ruby caught sight of herself in the bathroom mirror. Dark circles shadowed her usually bright eyes, and her hair was a tangled mess. For a moment, she didn't recognize the harried woman staring back at her.

"Come on, Rubes," she said to her reflection. "You've got this. Today's the day things turn around." It was the same pep talk she'd given herself every morning for months. Maybe if she said it enough times, it would come true.

The pep talk might have been more convincing if she could find two matching socks.

After a fruitless search, Ruby resigned herself to an odd pair—one faded blue, one bright pink. As she pulled them on, she shook her head in quiet amusement.

Her mother would be mortified if she could see her now. Margaret Whitaker's voice echoed in her head: *A put-together appearance is the first step to a put-together life, Ruby Jean.*

Well, Mom, Ruby thought, *I guess my life is as mismatched as my socks.*

The clatter of mail falling through the slot jolted Ruby from her reverie. Bills, no doubt. More reminders of all the ways she was falling short. She considered ignoring them, adding to the pile on her entry table that had become a poor man's filing system. But something—stubbornness, maybe, or a last vestige of responsibility—made her crouch down to gather the scattered envelopes.

Credit card offer—ha! Utility bill—double ha! Ruby frowned, her fingers brushing against an envelope that stood out from the rest. Thicker paper, almost like parchment, with her name and address written in elegant, unfamiliar handwriting. No return address.

Her curiosity piqued, she tore it open, unfolding the letter inside. Her eyes skimmed the first lines, and the noise of the city faded away. The world narrowed to the words on the page:

Dear Ms. Whitaker,

We are writing to inform you that you have been named the sole beneficiary of the estate of your uncle, Peter Larkin...

Ruby's breath caught in her throat. Uncle Peter? The black sheep of the family, more myth than man? She'd met him a handful of times, each encounter leaving her with the impression of a man who lived life by his own rules, consequences be damned.

As she read on, the words blurred together. Estate. Aspen Cove, Colorado. It was all hers.

Ruby sank onto her secondhand couch, the springs groaning in protest. Her mind raced, memories surfacing of the few times she'd encountered her enigmatic uncle. His booming laugh at family gatherings and the way he'd wink at her, as if they shared some grand secret, were vivid in her memory. How he always seemed to appear and disappear like some magician, leaving a wake of wild stories and raised eyebrows.

"And now, apparently, there was a house in Colorado." What the hell was she supposed to do with that?

Her phone buzzed, the screen lighting up with a

reminder: Video call with Client From Hell in 15 minutes. Ruby glanced from the phone to the letter and back again, feeling as if she were on the edge of a cliff. On one side, the familiar chaos of her current life. On the other ... what? Freedom? Adventure? Financial ruin in a more scenic location?

As Ruby stared at the letter, a spark of something long dormant stirred to life in her chest. Hope rose within her, sweet and unexpected.

Ruby read the letter again, her heart pounding. The legalese swam before her eyes, but a few key phrases stood out: "sole beneficiary," and "debt-free."

She let out a laugh that sounded unhinged, even to her own ears. Debt-free. When was the last time anything in her life had been that?

Her gaze drifted to the corkboard above her desk, covered in Post-it notes of varying degrees of urgency. "Call Mom," said one, the edges curling from age. Another read "Pitch new clients!!!" with enough exclamation points to betray her desperation. And in the center, written in bold red marker: "MAKE RENT OR ELSE."

Ruby's landlord, a mustachioed man with all the charm of a hungry piranha, had made it clear that his patience— and her tenancy—was wearing thin. One more late payment and she'd be out on the street, portfolio and student debt in tow.

But now ... now she had options. A lifeline, thrown to her by an uncle she hardly knew.

She pulled out her phone, fingers hovering over the search bar. What did one search for in this situation? "What to do when you unexpectedly inherit property from your estranged uncle?" Somehow, she doubted there'd be a wikiHow article for that.

Instead, she typed in "Aspen Cove, Colorado." The search results loaded, revealing images that belonged on a postcard: majestic mountains with snow-capped peaks, lush forests of pine and aspen, and a quaint town center with buildings that looked like they'd been plucked from a movie set.

It was beautiful and peaceful. The complete antithesis of her cramped apartment with its view of a brick wall and a perpetually overflowing dumpster.

As Ruby scrolled through the images, a memory surfaced. She was ten years old, spending a rare afternoon with Uncle Peter during one of his infrequent visits. They were sitting on the back porch, Ruby nursing a scraped knee from a failed attempt at skateboarding.

"You know, Ruby Tuesday," Uncle Peter had said, using the nickname only he ever called her, "there's a whole world out there beyond these suburbs. Mountains that touch the sky, forests so quiet you can hear your own heartbeat. That's where the real magic happens."

She'd rolled her eyes then, in the way every preteen could. "Whatever, Uncle Peter. I'm gonna live in the big city and be a famous artist."

He looked at me with a gentle, knowing smile. "Maybe so, kiddo. But remember, sometimes the universe has other plans. And those plans? They're usually better than anything we could dream up ourselves."

The memory faded, leaving Ruby feeling a heaviness she couldn't shake. Had Uncle Peter somehow known she'd end up needing this escape hatch? Or was it just one of life's strange coincidences?

In a few minutes, she'd have to pull herself together and pretend to care about website color schemes and font choices.

But for the first time in months—maybe years—a spark of excitement took hold within Ruby. A sense of possibility. She had choices now. She could sell the property, pay off her debts, maybe even squirrel away enough for a fresh start somewhere new. Or...

Or she could go to Aspen Cove. See this place for herself. Breathe in that mountain air Uncle Peter had raved about, walk in his footsteps, maybe even understand why he'd left her this unexpected gift.

The responsible thing would be to call a real estate agent, get the property assessed, put it on the market. That's what her mother would advise. It's what any sane person would do.

But Ruby was tired of being responsible. Tired of playing it safe and ending up miserable anyway.

Her fingers hovered over her laptop, itching to search for flights to Colorado. It was crazy. Impulsive. Potentially disastrous.

It was what she needed.

The video call notification popped up on her screen, her client's name flashing insistently. Ruby took a deep breath, squaring her shoulders. One last job, she told herself. One last dive into the world of hex codes and design. And then ... well, then it would be time for an adventure.

As she clicked to accept the call, a lightness spread through Ruby, more freeing than anything she'd experienced in years. She greeted her client on the screen, the mismatched socks on her feet seeming less like a mistake and more like a sign.

"Good morning!" she said, surprising herself with her enthusiasm. "Before we get started, I should let you know— this will be my last project for a while. I'm taking a ... sabbatical."

The word tasted foreign on her tongue, but not unpleasant. As her client sputtered in confusion, Ruby's amusement grew.

Sometimes the universe does have other plans, she thought. And Uncle Peter? Wherever you are, I hope you're enjoying the show.

CHAPTER TWO

The ancient truck groaned as Becket Shepherd navigated another bend in the winding country road, its weathered frame a testament to years of hard use and makeshift repairs. He squinted against the harsh winter sunlight, his calloused hands gripping the steering wheel with a tension that spoke of more than just difficult driving conditions.

Becket, a third-generation rancher from eastern Colorado, never imagined he'd be in this situation. Six months ago, he had a thriving goat farm, a decent plot of land he rented from old Mr. Johnson, and a future that seemed as solid as the Rocky Mountains on the horizon. But then the drought hit, worse than anyone had seen in decades. The pastures dried up, feed prices skyrocketed, and Mr. Johnson, facing his own financial crisis, had to sell the land.

Just like that, Becket was without a home for his beloved herd. He'd sold off what he could—his equipment, his truck, and even his prized guitar, replacing the truck with a wheezing relic. But parting with the core of his herd was out of the question: five nannies, two billies, and a handful of kids. They were more than livestock; they were family.

So here he was, a nomad in his own state, driving from town to town, looking for temporary grazing arrangements, odd jobs, anything to keep his goats fed and his dream of rebuilding his farm alive.

To either side of the road, barren fields stretched out like a bleak canvas, the once-lush landscape now a patchwork of brittle brown and faded yellow. The persistent drought had transformed the region into a harsh, unforgiving terrain that seemed to mock the idea of life and growth.

A restless bleating from the trailer behind him pulled at Becket's attention. He didn't need to see them to know what was happening. The goats were getting hungry. Again. And among those familiar voices, he could pick out one in particular—a lower, more insistent call that made his heart clench with worry.

Daisy. His prize Nubian nanny, heavy with kid and due any day now.

"Hang in there, old girl," he said, though he knew she couldn't hear him over the rumble of the engine. "We'll find you something good to eat. You and that little one of yours."

Becket's fingers tightened on the steering wheel. The pregnancy had been a surprise, coming late in the season when he least expected it. Now, it was both a blessing and a complication. Daisy needed extra nutrition, a safe place to kid, and Becket was running out of both time and options to provide them. Still, he thought that all things happen for a reason.

He pressed down on the accelerator, a new urgency driving his search. This wasn't just about keeping the herd fed anymore—he needed to secure a future for the tiny life

Daisy carried. Her bleats, more demanding than the others, served as a constant reminder of the precious cargo he was responsible for.

Becket's eyes flicked to the fuel gauge, and his jaw tightened. The needle hovered just above empty, a visual reminder of his dwindling resources. He'd been driving for hours, crisscrossing the county in search of any patch of land that might offer some respite for his hungry herd. So far, his quest had been fruitless.

As he drove, memories of better times passed through his mind. He remembered lush, green pastures where his goats had grazed, their coats gleaming in the summer sun. He thought of the local farmers' markets where he'd sold his goat cheese, basking in the praise of customers who declared it the best they'd ever tasted.

But those days seemed like a distant dream now. The drought had changed everything, transforming the once-thriving agricultural community into a community struggling for survival. Many of Becket's neighbors had already given up on selling their land and moving on to greener pastures—literally and figuratively.

Becket gritted his teeth, pushing away the wave of misery that threatened to overwhelm him. He wasn't ready to give up. Not yet. There had to be a solution, some way to keep his small enterprise afloat until the rains and snow returned.

As he rounded another bend, a modest farmhouse came into view. It sat back from the road. The house itself was unremarkable, a basic build with siding and a small barn. But what caught Becket's attention was the yard.

Where most properties in the area were brown and lifeless, this yard was a riot of green. Weeds of every description had taken over, growing unchecked in the absence of regular maintenance. Becket slowed the truck, his eyes widening as he took in the unexpected oasis.

He pulled over to the side of the road, letting the engine idle as he stared at the overgrown property. The goats in the trailer perked up, their fussing taking on a more urgent tone as they sensed the proximity of food.

"Well, I'll be damned," Becket said. It wasn't pretty, and it certainly wasn't the kind of grazing land he'd been hoping for, but it was green. And where there was green, there was hope.

As he sat there, an idea began to take shape in the back of his mind. The sounds from the trailer had quieted somewhat, but he could still hear Daisy's occasional low call. It spurred his thoughts, adding fuel to the spark of his budding idea. If he could make this work, it wouldn't just mean survival for the herd—it could mean a safe, well-fed haven for Daisy to have her kid.

What if, instead of searching for open pastures that no longer existed, he used the goats to clear overgrown properties like this one? People might not have the time, energy, or equipment to deal with yards that had gotten out of control —especially in the winter. But his goats? They'd make short work of those weeds.

The more Becket thought about it, the more excited he became. This wasn't just about survival anymore—this was an opportunity. He could offer his goats as a natural, eco-friendly landscaping service. In a place like this, where the drought had left everyone with little to work with, it might be exactly what folks needed.

Energized by the possibility, Becket shifted the truck back into gear and continued down the road, his mind racing with plans. He just needed a way to get the word out—maybe talk to a few locals, or better yet, find someone who knew the area and could spread the word for him.

A few miles later, he spotted a small strip mall nestled at the intersection of two country roads. Most of the storefronts were empty, their windows dark and uninviting. But one shop stood out, its lights on and a small "OPEN" sign hanging in the window.

Becket's eyes flicked to the familiar logo on the sign in front of the small realty office. Silver Springs Realty. It was the same one he'd seen on the property he'd just passed—the overgrown yard that had sparked his idea. A surge of possibility coursed through him. If anyone knew how many neglected lots like that were scattered around the area, it would be a real estate agent.

He pulled into the mostly empty parking lot, the truck's brakes squealing in protest as he came to a stop. As he climbed out of the cab, he caught his reflection in the truck's side mirror. His face was lined with worry and fatigue, his clothes dusty from days spent more in the fields than in his house. He ran a hand through his unruly hair, trying to make himself look a bit more presentable.

"You can do this, Shepherd," he muttered to himself. "It's just another sales pitch. No different than hawking cheese at the market."

But as he approached the office door, doubt began to creep in. What if they laughed him out of the place? What if this idea was as dried up and useless as the fields he'd been searching for all day?

Becket hesitated, his hand on the door handle. Behind him, he heard the goats in the trailer, a reminder of why he was here. Of why he couldn't give up.

Taking a deep breath, he pushed open the door and stepped inside.

The office was small and cluttered, with stacks of papers covering every available surface. The walls were lined with photos of properties—houses that had seen better days, parcels of land that looked more suited to tumbleweeds than crops. The air smelled of stale coffee and desperation.

Behind a desk piled high with folders sat a woman Becket guessed to be in her late fifties. Her salt-and-pepper hair was pulled back in a severe bun, and she peered at him over the top of reading glasses perched precariously on the end of her nose.

"Can I help you?" she asked, her tone suggesting she hoped the answer was no.

Becket cleared his throat, suddenly aware of how out of place he must look. "Afternoon, ma'am," he said. "Name's Becket Shepherd. I was hoping to talk to you about a business proposition."

The woman—her nameplate identified her as Marge Gunderson—raised an eyebrow. "Mr. Shepherd, if you're looking to list a property, I'm afraid I've got some bad news for you. Market's deader than a doornail these days. Drought's seen to that."

Becket shook his head, taking a step closer to the desk. "No, ma'am, I'm not looking to sell. I'm here to offer a service. One that might help with some of those harder-to-sell properties."

Marge leaned back in her chair, curiosity replacing the initial dismissal in her eyes. "I'm listening."

Taking a deep breath, Becket launched into his pitch. He told her about his goats, about how effective they were at clearing overgrown land. He painted a picture of transformed properties, of happy homeowners freed from the burden of unmanageable yards.

As he spoke, he could see the skepticism in Marge's eyes giving way to interest. When he finished, she was silent for a long moment, studying him with an intensity that made him want to fidget.

"Goats," she said with a hint of amusement in her voice. "You're proposing to solve our landscaping problems with goats."

Becket nodded, standing his ground. "Yes, ma'am. I know it sounds strange, but I'm willing to prove it works. I'll do the first job for free—any property you choose. If you're not satisfied with the results, you don't owe me a thing."

Marge considered this, tapping a pen against her desk. "And what makes you think people around here would go for something like this? Folks tend to be set in their ways, you know."

"Times are tough," Becket replied, his voice low and earnest. "People are looking for solutions, for ways to make do with what they have. My goats offer an eco-friendly, cost-effective alternative to traditional landscaping. And in this drought? Every bit of green we can use matters."

As Becket gave Marge his details, a particularly sharp bleat came from outside. He winced, recognizing Daisy's voice. "Sorry about that," he said, glancing nervously at the window. "One of my girls is expecting. Makes her a bit vocal sometimes."

Marge's eyebrows rose. "Expecting? You mean you've got a pregnant goat in that trailer?"

Becket nodded, a mixture of pride and worry crossing his face. "Yes, ma'am. Daisy's due in a few weeks. It's why I'm so keen on finding new grazing options. She needs the extra nutrition, you see."

Something in Marge's expression softened. "Well, now," she said, her tone gentler than before. "That does put a different spin on things, doesn't it?" She tapped her pen against the desk, thinking. "Tell you what, Mr. Shepherd. I've got a property on the edge of town. The old Wilson place. Been empty for months, and the yard's a mess. Why don't you take your goats over there. Consider it a trial run."

Becket's heart leapt. "Really? The Wilson place?" He nodded as recognition dawned on his face. "Yeah, I know it. Passed by it a few times—it's been looking rough for a while." He grinned. "My goats will make short work of that yard."

Marge waved off his thanks. "Don't make me regret this. And Mr. Shepherd? Make sure that mama goat of yours is taken care of. Times are hard enough without bringing new life into the world unprepared."

Relief washed over Becket as he thanked Marge again. There were no guarantees, but at least it was a start. As he turned to leave, Marge called out to him.

"Mr. Shepherd?"

He paused at the door, turning to look back.

Marge took a moment before speaking. "It's not an easy time to be starting something new around here, but I admire your determination. Best of luck to you."

Becket dipped his head in acknowledgment. "Thank you, ma'am. I reckon we could all use a little luck these days."

As he stepped back out into the cold afternoon air, a weight seemed to lift from Becket's shoulders. He wasn't out of the woods yet, not by a long shot. But for the first time in weeks, he had a direction, a purpose beyond mere survival.

He climbed back into his truck, the familiar creak of the door a comforting sound. As he started the engine, he listened to the chorus of bleats from the trailer, picking out Daisy's distinctive voice among them.

"Well," he said, a note of determination in his voice, "looks like we might be going into the landscaping business."

The goats bleated in response. It might not have been much, but it was a plan. And sometimes, that small step was enough to keep going.

As he pulled out of the parking lot and back onto the dusty road, Becket's mind was already racing with the next steps. He needed to prepare the goats for their new job, maybe rig up some portable fencing. He'd have to work on his pitch, fine-tune it for different kinds of properties.

Becket and his goats were virtually nomads, left without a place to call home. The drought had already taken so much from them, and he knew this project needed to succeed—not just for himself, but for his animals. This crazy idea might be their first step toward reclaiming some stability, a chance to take back even a little of what they'd lost.

Becket drove on, the setting sun painting the barren landscape in shades of gold and red. Tomorrow would bring new challenges, new doubts. But for now, he allowed himself to feel something he hadn't in a long time: hope.

CHAPTER THREE

Ruby's rental car crawled along the winding mountain road, her knuckles white on the steering wheel. The GPS had given up miles ago, leaving her with nothing but the crumpled letter from the lawyer and her uncle's cryptic directions. This was nothing like navigating Chicago's grid system, where even the most directionally challenged could find their way.

"Take a left at the big oak that looks like it's giving the finger to everyone who enters," Ruby muttered, reading aloud from Uncle Peter's note that was included in the letter. "Then right at the rock shaped like Nixon's nose. What the hell?"

She squinted at the passing landscape, feeling more lost by the second. "Great. I've gone from the Magnificent Mile to a scavenger hunt designed by a stoned park ranger."

Just as she was about to give up and turn around, Ruby spotted it—an ancient oak tree with one gnarled branch reaching skyward in what could be described as a wooden middle finger.

"Well, I'll be damned," she said with a shake of her

"

head, taking the left. "Uncle Peter, your sense of humor is ... something else."

A few minutes later, a lumpy boulder appeared on the roadside, its profile bearing an uncanny resemblance to the 37th president.

"Nixon's nose. Check," Ruby said, shaking her head as she turned right.

As she rounded the next bend, a wooden sign appeared: "Welcome to Aspen Cove—Population: Growing!"

Ruby snorted. "Charming."

She passed a small green space with a gazebo—Hope Park, according to a quaint little sign—before Main Street came into view. And boy, was that a generous name for it. The whole town center was essentially one block. It made Ruby's trendy Wicker Park neighborhood back in Chicago look positively metropolitan.

"Alright, Uncle Peter," Ruby sighed, "let's see what kind of time capsule you've dropped me into."

She crawled down Main Street, taking in the sights. On one side: a corner store that wore its history on its sleeve, its faded sign hinting at decades of stories. Next to it, a pharmacy with a blinking sign declaring "The Doctor Is In," a veterinary clinic, and a diner proudly proclaiming itself as "Maisey's."

Across the street, she spotted a sheriff's office, Bishop's Brewhouse—a place that, given the size of the town, was likely just some guy named Bishop brewing hooch in his bathtub—along with Bishop's Bait and Tackle and a bakery simply labeled "B's Bakery." Ruby decided "B's" must stand for "Bewildering," given its strange proximity to a bait shop.

"This town has more B's than a spelling bee," Ruby muttered, pulling into a parking spot in front of the pharmacy where she was supposed to find a Doc Parker.

She sat, gathering her courage. "Okay, Rubes. You've dealt with Lake Shore Drive during rush hour. You can handle a small-town pharmacist."

The bell above the door rang as she entered, the sound cheerful despite the sterile smell of rubbing alcohol that hit her as soon as she stepped inside. The interior was an odd blend of modern pharmacy essentials and small-town general store clutter. It was nothing like the sleek, efficient CVS on every Chicago corner.

Behind the counter sat a man who looked to be in his seventies or eighties, his nose buried in a newspaper. His thick, white mustache, which could easily rival Tom Selleck's, twitched as he glanced up at her entrance.

"Excuse me," Ruby said as she approached the counter. "I'm Ruby Whitaker, and I'm supposed to meet someone named Doc Parker?"

The old man's eyebrows shot up, a glimmer of recognition in his eyes. "Well, well. I've been wondering when you'd show up. Peter's niece, gracing us with her presence."

"You've been expecting me?" Ruby asked, surprised.

Doc's mustache twitched in what might have been a smirk. "In a town this size, honey, we expect the sun to rise, the corn to grow, and Peter Larkin's niece to eventually turn up. I'm Doc Parker."

"Oh," Ruby said, taken aback. "Well, nice to meet you. The lawyer said you'd have the keys to Uncle Peter's place?"

"That I do," Doc replied, rummaging under the counter. "Peter also made me promise to give you the grand tour of Aspen Cove. God help me." He let out a long-suffering sigh. "The things I do for that old coot, even after he's gone."

Despite his grumbling, Doc heaved himself up from his chair and flipped the "Back in 5 minutes" sign on the door.

"Come on then, let's get this over with. And don't say I never did anything for you."

As they walked outside, Doc's commentary blended snarky observations with fatherly advice. "That there's Cove Cuts," he said, gesturing to a hair salon. "Marina runs it. She gives cuts so good they ought to be illegal—but lucky for her, she's married to the sheriff. Word of advice: don't mention Chicago pizza around her unless you want an hour-long lecture on why New York-style is superior."

Ruby tried to hold on to her big-city skepticism, but there was something about Doc's gruff humor and the absurdity of it all that—dare she say it—was undeniably endearing. This world was far removed from the fast-paced, often impersonal interactions she was used to in Chicago.

"And if you're hungry, B's Bakery has the best muffins in town, thanks to Katie. But for the best meal ever, head over to Maisey's for the blue plate special. Just don't tell my Lovey I said that—I'd hate to hurt her feelings."

Doc pointed to a cozy-looking establishment across the street. "That there is Bishop's Brewhouse. You can find me there every afternoon at four for my daily beer. Can't get a figure like this drinking Diet Coke," he added, patting his belly.

As they headed back to her car, Ruby took in the town's holiday display—twinkling lights strung across storefronts and wreaths hanging on every door. Doc handed her a set of keys that looked like they could have been forged in the days of the Gold Rush.

"And for heaven's sake," Doc added, his tone softening, "if you need anything—and I mean anything—you come see me. Peter would haunt me till my dying day if I didn't look out for you. Not that I'm volunteering to be your surrogate father or anything, mind you. I've got enough on my plate keeping this town from falling apart."

Ruby was oddly touched by the gruff offer. "Thanks, Doc. Can you point me in the right direction to Uncle Peter's place?"

"It's just up Pansy Lane," he said, pointing down a side street. "Can't miss it. It's the one that looks like Mother Nature is trying to reclaim it for the forest."

Ruby raised an eyebrow. "Sounds … delightful. I'm guessing there's no HOA here like back in Lincoln Park."

"Peter always said he was just 'cultivating wilderness,'" Doc said, amused. "You might want to bring a machete."

As Ruby climbed back into her car, Doc leaned in, his expression softening. "Listen, I know this isn't what you expected. It must feel like you've landed on another planet after Chicago. But give it a chance, will you? Aspen Cove has a way of growing on you."

"Like mold?" Ruby quipped.

"More like a persistent ivy," Doc winked. "But in a good way."

As she drove down Pansy Lane, each house looking more Norman Rockwell than the last, Ruby had the distinct impression that she'd stepped into another world. Finally, she spotted it—a house that looked like it had seen better days, sometime around the Lincoln administration. The porch sagged like it was tired of standing, and the paint peeled like it was trying to escape. But the yard … the yard was a riot of green, plants of all kinds growing in a chaotic tangle that seemed to defy the drought-stricken landscape around it.

"Well," Ruby sighed, killing the engine, "home sweet home. Or at least, somebody's idea of it." She glanced at her phone, relieved to see one bar of signal. "Thank God. At least I'm not cut off from civilization."

She walked up to the porch, each step creaking ominously. As she fitted the key into the lock, a strange feeling washed over her. It wasn't quite excitement, wasn't quite dread. It was ... possibility.

The door swung open with a groan, revealing a dim interior cluttered with shapes Ruby couldn't quite make out. She fumbled for a light switch, her fingers brushing against what seemed to be stacks of paper. She found the switch and flicked it on.

Light flooded the room, and Ruby's jaw dropped. Every surface, from floor to ceiling, was covered in ... stuff. Boxes upon boxes stacked precariously high, creating narrow pathways through the chaos. Old magazines, antique furniture, gadgets she couldn't even begin to identify—it was like stepping into the world's most claustrophobic antique shop.

"Oh, Uncle Peter," she muttered, eyeing a tower of hatboxes that looked ready to topple at any moment, "what in the world have you been collecting all these years?"

Ruby picked her way through the clutter, managing to clear a small space on what she assumed was once a couch. Sinking down onto the dusty cushions, she pulled out her phone and dialed her mother's number.

"Mom? Yeah, I'm here. It's ... well, it's something else."

Her mother's voice crackled through the speaker. "Oh, honey. I was afraid of that. Peter always was a bit of a pack rat. You should call a real estate agent right away. And maybe someone with a dumpster."

Ruby's eyes scanned the room as her mother spoke. Each pile of junk looked less like trash and more like snippets of Uncle Peter's life. Memories. Stories. Adventures.

There was a reason he had been estranged from the family. He was strange.

"I don't know, Mom," Ruby said. "I mean, yes, it's a mess, but ... this was Uncle Peter's life. It deserves a little respect, doesn't it?"

Her mother sighed. "Well, it's your inheritance. Just don't let sentiment cloud your judgment. You can't live in a museum of old junk."

After saying goodbye, Ruby stood up, determined to at least get a full tour of her new ... home? Museum? Obstacle course? As she made her way to the kitchen, she spotted something that made her do a double-take.

There, on a cluttered counter, sat an actual, honest-to-god landline phone. And beneath it, a thick book that Ruby recognized from the depths of her childhood memories.

"Is that ... a phone book?" she marveled, picking up the relic with a mixture of amusement and awe. "I didn't think these even existed anymore."

Chuckling to herself, Ruby began to flip through the yellowed pages. Her eyes scanned the listings, looking for real estate agents. There were no options but Doc in the area.

Ruby's eyebrows shot up as she read Doc's ad: "Doc Parker: Your One-Stop Shop for What Ails Ya (And Your House)!

- Medicine dispensed with a smile
- Real estate sold with a wink
- Free lollipop with every transaction (house or prescription)
- Special discount if you need both at once!"

Ruby snorted, shaking her head. "Right, because what

this town needs is a man wearing even more hats. I think I'll let the good doctor stick to saving lives and enjoying his afternoon beer."

She continued flipping through the pages, muttering to herself, "Come on, there's got to be a real professional around here somewhere."

Her eyes landed on an ad that stood out from the rest. It was larger than the others, with a bold headline: "Silver Springs Realty—We Turn Houses into Homes and Hoarders' Dens into Gold Mines!"

Her finger traced down to the contact information: Gunderson, Marge—Silver Springs Realty, serving Silver Springs and surrounding areas.

"Huh," Ruby said. "Not even a local agency. I guess beggars can't be choosers when it comes to unloading houses full of junk."

Ruby hesitated, her hand hovering over her cell phone. This was it—the moment of truth. One call, and she'd set in motion the process of selling Uncle Peter's house. Of erasing this small piece of him from the world.

But as her eyes drifted over the piles of memories surrounding her, a twinge of ... something tugged at Ruby. Curiosity? Responsibility? Or maybe just the nagging feeling that there was more to this inheritance than met the eye.

"Oh, what the hell," she muttered, setting her phone down without dialing. "One night won't hurt. I can always call Marge in the morning."

As if in agreement, a stack of books chose that moment to lose its battle with gravity, toppling to the floor with a resounding crash. Ruby jumped, then burst out laughing.

"Alright, Uncle Peter," she said to the cluttered room. "I

hear you. Let's see what kind of adventure you've left for me."

CHAPTER FOUR

Becket Shepherd steered his truck onto the overgrown driveway of the old Wilson place, his heart pounding with hope and anxiety. The property Marge Gunderson had offered for his goat landscaping trial was just the lifeline he and his herd needed. Now, if the universe would cooperate for once.

Becket glanced in the rearview mirror. "Hang in there, Daisy. We've got a couple weeks to go yet. Try not to pop that kid out before Christmas, okay?"

He pulled to a stop and climbed out of the cab, wincing as his boots sank into the unexpectedly soft ground. The late afternoon sun cast long shadows across the overgrown but oddly green field—a striking oasis in the otherwise parched landscape. "Well, gang," he muttered, eyeing the wild tangle of weeds and grass that thrived against all odds, "looks like we've got our work cut out for us."

Becket had just started to lower the trailer ramp when the wail of a police siren cut through the air. He froze, one hand on the trailer latch, the other instinctively reaching to smooth down his unruly hair. "Ah, hell," he muttered, watching a Silver Springs Police cruiser pull up behind his truck. "Just what we need. A welcoming committee."

As the car door opened, Becket straightened up, trying his best to look like a respectable businessman and not a vagrant goatherder. It wasn't easy, given the circumstances.

"Evening, officer," Becket called out, aiming for casual and missing by a mile. "Lovely evening for a bit of ... goat herding, wouldn't you say?"

The officer approached, hand resting casually on his belt. "This is private property, sir. Would you care to explain what is going on here?"

Becket's mind raced. How could he possibly explain this situation without sounding insane? "Well, you see, it's a funny story..."

He launched into an explanation about his meeting with Marge, the landscaping idea, and his hopes to keep things going until at least Christmas. "You see, officer, Daisy there—" he pointed to the pregnant goat, who chose that moment to let out a loud, accusatory bleat, "—she's due to kid around Christmas. I'm just trying to find a way to keep us all going until then. Marge Gunderson gave me permission to use this property as a trial run."

The officer's eyebrows shot up. "Marge Gunderson? The realtor?" His tone was skeptical, bordering on dismissive.

"That's right." Becket nodded, hope rising in his chest. "You can call her to verify. She should still be in her office at this hour."

The officer's face hardened. "Sir, I'm going to need you to step away from the trailer. Do you have any documentation to prove this arrangement?"

Becket's heart sank. "Well, no, not exactly. It was more of a verbal agreement, you see..."

"A verbal agreement," the officer repeated flatly. "To bring a herd of goats onto private property at dusk."

"When you put it like that, it does sound a bit crazy," Becket admitted, his voice strained. "But I swear, I'm telling the truth. These goats, they're all I've got left. I'm just trying to make a fresh start here."

The officer sighed, torn between skepticism and a hint of sympathy. "Mr...?"

"Shepherd. Becket Shepherd."

"Of course it is," the officer muttered. "Mr. Shepherd, I can't allow you to stay here without verifying your story. I'm going to have to ask you to pack up and move along."

Panic rose in Becket's chest. "But officer, please. I've got nowhere else to go. These goats need to eat, and Daisy's due soon. Can't you just ... I don't know, give me a chance to sort this out with Marge?"

The officer studied him for a long moment, then glanced at the herd of goats, some of whom were already eyeing the overgrown grass eagerly. He shook his head. "Alright. Here's what we're going to do. I'm going to call Ms. Gunderson right now to verify your story. If she backs you up, you can stay. If not, you and your ... landscaping crew will need to move on immediately. Understood?"

Relief flooded through Becket. "Yes, sir. Thank you. I promise, everything will check out."

The officer stepped away to make the call, leaving Becket to wait anxiously. After what seemed like an eternity, he returned.

"Well, it seems Ms. Gunderson does indeed recall your ... unusual arrangement. You're free to stay for now, but consider yourself on notice. Any complaints from the neighbors and you're out. Clear?"

"Crystal clear, officer. Thank you," Becket said, trying not to sound too giddy with relief.

As the officer turned to leave, he paused, looking back at Becket with amusement. "And Mr. Shepherd? This town's seen its share of crazy schemes, but goat landscaping? That's a new one. For your sake, I hope it works out."

Watching the cruiser drive away, Becket let out a breath he didn't realize he'd been holding. He turned back to his goats, Daisy front and center, eyeing him with what he swore was judgment.

"Don't look at me like that," he told her, reaching out to scratch behind her ears. "This was your idea, remember? You're the one who decided to get knocked up at the most inconvenient time possible."

Daisy responded by attempting to eat his shirt.

"Alright, alright," Becket said, gently pushing her away. "I get it. Less talking, more setting up. We've got a job to do."

Luckily, he'd had the foresight to load the portable fencing in his truck that morning, knowing the goats would need an enclosure. As he began to unload it, Becket ran through his mental checklist. He knew from experience that his herd could clear about a quarter acre per day if the vegetation wasn't too dense. Looking at the overgrown field before him, he estimated it would take at least a week to make a real dent.

"Okay, gang," he said, addressing his herd of nannies, billies, and kids as he set up the first section of fencing. "Here's the deal. We're going to tackle this place in sections. Can't have you eating everything in sight on the first night, or we'll be out of a job before we start."

He raised an eyebrow as the goats bleated back. "I

know, I know. You're all overachievers. But trust me, pacing ourselves is key here."

As the sun began to set, Becket finished setting up a modest enclosure, enough to keep the goats busy for the night without decimating the entire property. He would move the fencing each day, which would allow the goats to systematically clear the land.

"There we go," he said, stepping back to admire his work. "Home sweet home, at least for tonight."

Becket let out a contented sigh as he watched them, pride swelling in his chest.

Despite everything, there was something deeply satisfying about seeing his herd do what they did best.

As the last light of day faded and stars began to twinkle above the overgrown field, Becket allowed himself a moment of quiet reflection. This wasn't where he'd expected to end up, but then again, life had a way of throwing curveballs.

"Well, gang," he said, watching his diverse herd settle into their work, "looks like we might just have a shot at this after all. Let's show Silver Springs what a bunch of goats can do."

He patted Daisy's side. "And you, mama, let's get through this job before you decide to add to our workforce, okay?"

As he set up his own modest camp for the night, a glimmer of hope sparked in Becket. It wasn't much, but it was a start. And who knew? Maybe by Christmas, this crazy scheme of his might just turn into the gift he and his goats so desperately needed.

"Merry almost-Christmas to us," he said as the goats munched, their chewing filling the night air. "Here's to new beginnings, one weed at a time."

CHAPTER FIVE

Ruby awoke with a start, momentarily disoriented by the unfamiliar surroundings. Sunlight streamed through dusty windows, illuminating the cluttered living room of Uncle Peter's house. She'd fallen asleep on the couch, surrounded by teetering piles of … well, everything. A spring dug into her back, and her neck ached from the awkward angle she'd been lying in.

"Right," she muttered, rubbing her eyes. "Inherited hoarder's paradise. Not a dream."

As she sat up, a cascade of papers slid off her lap onto the floor. Ruby sighed, reaching down to gather them. Her hand paused as she caught sight of a faded photograph peeking out from the pile.

It was Uncle Peter, much younger than she'd ever known him, standing proudly in front of a vintage car. His arm was around a woman Ruby didn't recognize, both of them looking happily at the camera. The woman's blonde hair caught the sunlight, and Uncle Peter was looking at her with unmistakable adoration.

"What other secrets are you hiding in here, Uncle Peter?" Ruby mused, setting the photo aside.

Her stomach growled, reminding her that she hadn't eaten since ... when? Yesterday's drive? With a groan, Ruby hauled herself off the couch and picked her way through the clutter towards what she hoped was the kitchen.

The scene that greeted her was somehow both what she expected and utterly surprising. Every surface was covered in mismatched kitchenware and what looked like souvenirs from every state fair in Colorado. It was as if a flea market had exploded and then been left to gather dust for a decade.

"Okay," Ruby said to the empty room, "let's see if there's anything edible in this ... museum of randomness."

She opened a cabinet, to be met with an avalanche of mismatched Tupperware. Dodging the falling plastic, Ruby laughed. "You never threw anything away, did you?"

After some rummaging, she managed to unearth a box of crackers that was slightly past its expiration date and a jar of peanut butter that looked safe enough. It wasn't a gourmet breakfast, but it would do.

As she picked at the stale crackers and peanut butter, Ruby's eyes drifted to the window. What she saw didn't quite line up with her expectations—or reality, for that matter. Beyond the property, the land looked thirsty, like the drought had sucked every last drop of life from the earth. But Uncle Peter's house? It was the complete opposite. The lawn was a riot of green, overgrown with wild vegetation and weeds that stood out like an oasis in the middle of a desert. It was as if this house had missed the memo about the drought entirely.

"Huh," she muttered, frowning. "I guess the mountains are different than I thought."

She had imagined getting here and seeing lush green

pines and underbrush that was just as vibrant. But when they call the Rockies the high desert, they weren't kidding. She made a mental note to brush up on the local geography. If she was going to sell this place, she'd need to know how to pitch it.

Ruby finished her crackers and peanut butter, washing them down with tap water from a glass she'd rinsed about five times, just to be safe. As she set the glass down, her eyes caught on a small leather-bound book wedged between a tacky ceramic rooster and what looked like a vintage cigarette dispenser.

Curiosity piqued, Ruby extracted the book. Its cover was worn soft with age and use. Opening it, she found pages filled with Uncle Peter's messy scrawl. It seemed to be some sort of journal.

"Well, Uncle Peter," Ruby said with a smirk, "what have you been hiding in here?"

She flipped it open to a random page and began to read:

June 15, 1985 - Note to self: Never try to charm two sisters at the same town picnic. Especially if one of them is married to the sheriff. On an unrelated note, the jailhouse sandwiches in Gold Gulch aren't half bad.

Ruby's eyebrows shot up. "Oh my," she laughed, flipping to another entry.

August 3, 1990 - Acquired a delightful antique barometer today. The seller seemed quite eager to part with it. Unrelated: Discovered I'm allergic to mercury. Currently writing this with my toes as my fingers are temporarily the size of sausages.

September 12, 1995 - Note to self: When a lady asks if her dress makes her look fat, 'Is the Pope Catholic?' is not an acceptable response. Even if you're in the middle of organizing your Vatican commemorative plate collection.

Ruby laughed out loud. Each page revealed a new facet of her uncle's colorful life—his flirtations, his misadventures, and his seemingly endless capacity for collecting the weird and wonderful.

"Oh," Ruby sighed, her voice caught between fondness and exasperation. "What am I supposed to do with all of this?"

The question hung in the air, unanswered. Ruby set the journal aside and stood up, stretching. She needed a shower and a change of clothes if she was going to face the day— and the daunting task of dealing with Uncle Peter's estate.

Navigating to the bathroom was an adventure in itself. Ruby had to squeeze past a tower of old *National Geographic* magazines, dodge a precariously balanced collection of what looked like vintage fishing lures, and almost tripped over a box labeled "Misc. Knick-Knacks Possibly Cursed???"

The bathroom, when she reached it, was thankfully less cluttered than the rest of the house. Still, it had its quirks. The shower curtain was adorned with a map of the world, with little red stickers stuck in various locations. Ruby wondered if these were places Uncle Peter had visited or places he'd planned to go.

As hot water sputtered from the showerhead, Ruby let out a sigh of relief. She stepped under the spray, letting it wash away the travel grime and the lingering disorientation of waking up in a strange place.

Under the steam and solitude of the shower, Ruby's mind wandered. What would her life in Chicago look like right now if she hadn't received that letter? Another day of juggling freelance gigs, dodging her landlord, and trying to ignore the gnawing feeling that she was just treading water?

Here, at least, she had ... what? A house full of junk and

a to-do list a mile long? But also, maybe, a chance at something different. Something she couldn't quite name yet.

Ruby shook her head, sending water droplets flying. "Get it together, Rubes," she said. "You're here to sell, not soul-search."

Feeling somewhat refreshed, Ruby stepped out of the shower and wrapped herself in a towel that had seen better days but smelled clean enough. She wiped the foggy mirror with her hand, studying her reflection.

The face that looked back at her seemed different somehow. Maybe it was the mountain air, or the strange sense of possibility that hung around this place like a mist. Or maybe she was just overtired and under-caffeinated.

Back in the bedroom, Ruby rummaged through her hastily packed suitcase for something to wear. She settled on jeans and a soft sweater—it looked cooler outside than she'd expected.

Dressed and marginally more put together, Ruby made her way back to the living room. It was time to face reality and call that real estate agent. She picked up her phone and the crumpled paper where she'd scribbled Marge Gunderson's number last night.

Ruby took a deep breath and dialed. After a few rings, a crisp, no-nonsense voice answered.

"Silver Springs Realty, Marge Gunderson speaking."

"Hi, Ms. Gunderson. This is Ruby Whitaker. I inherited a property in Aspen Cove from my uncle, Peter Larkin, and I was hoping you could help me sell it."

There was a pause on the other end of the line. "Peter Larkin's place? Well, honey, that's quite a ... unique property. Why don't I come take a look? I can be there in about an hour."

Ruby agreed, feeling a sense of anxiety. An hour. She

glanced around the cluttered living room. There was no way she could make this place presentable in an hour. Or a week, for that matter.

True to her word, Marge arrived precisely an hour later. Ruby watched from the porch as a meticulously maintained vintage Cadillac pulled up in front of the house. Marge Gunderson stepped out, every inch the professional in a smart blazer and practical shoes.

"Well," Marge said, surveying the overgrown yard with a raised eyebrow, "I can see we've got our work cut out for us."

Ruby led Marge through the house, wincing at every 'hmm' and 'I see' that escaped the realtor's lips. By the time they'd made it through all the rooms—or at least, all the rooms they could access without the aid of a search and rescue team—Ruby was thoroughly demoralized.

Marge turned to her, her expression showing both sympathy and determination. "I'm not going to sugarcoat it. Before we can even think about listing this place, we've got some work to do. A lot of work."

Ruby's heart sank. "How much work are we talking about?"

"Well, for starters, we need to declutter. Significantly." Marge's gaze swept over the crowded room. "You might think about getting a dumpster."

Ruby groaned. Her mother had suggested the same thing. "Great. Anything else?"

"The yard needs taming. It's a jungle out there." Marge rummaged in her purse and pulled out a business card. She scribbled a number on the back. "This guy, Becket Shepherd, he can take care of the yard. Might even do it for free."

Ruby took the card, frowning. "For free? Why would anyone do that?"

Marge shrugged. "He's got an ... unconventional approach. Give him a call. Trust me, you'll need all the help you can get."

As Marge headed back to her car, she turned to Ruby with a sympathetic smile. "Don't look so overwhelmed. Rome wasn't built in a day, and Peter Larkin's house won't be sold in one either. We'll get there."

Ruby watched Marge drive away, the business card feeling heavy in her hand. She looked at the number scrawled on the back. Becket Shepherd. She wondered what someone with a name like that might look like. Was he old and grizzled, or young and ruggedly handsome? And what kind of person did yard work for free?

As she headed back into the house, Ruby couldn't shake the feeling that she was in way over her head. But what choice did she have? If she wanted to sell this place—and she did, she reminded herself—she had a lot of work ahead of her.

"Well, Uncle Peter," she muttered, eyeing a precariously balanced stack of old magazines, "I hope you're enjoying the show. Because this is going to be one hell of a cleanup job."

With a sigh, Ruby picked up her phone again. Time to call about that dumpster. And maybe give this Becket Shepherd a try. After all, if he was willing to work for free, who was she to argue?

As she dialed, Ruby wondered what other surprises Aspen Cove had in store for her. Something told her that taming Uncle Peter's jungle of a yard was just the beginning.

Something warm and decidedly goat-like was nudging Becket's face. He groaned, trying to burrow deeper into his sleeping bag, but the insistent prodding continued. The crisp morning air nipped at his nose, reminding him that he was indeed sleeping outside in a field.

"Alright, alright, I'm up," he mumbled, cracking open one eye to find himself nose-to-nose with Houdini, his craftiest billy goat. The goat's breath smelled of fresh greenery and trouble. "Wait a minute..."

Becket bolted upright, his sleeping bag sliding off his chest. Houdini shouldn't be here. Houdini should be in the makeshift pen with the rest of the herd, safely contained on the Wilson property.

"Aw, hell," he muttered, scrambling to his feet. He'd spent the night sleeping under the stars, wanting to keep an eye on his goats in their new temporary home. Fat lot of good that did.

As he stood up, stretching out the kinks from a night on the hard ground, Becket's jaw dropped. The ramshackle enclosure he'd cobbled together yesterday evening from portable fencing and spare bits of rope was in shambles. Daisy, his pregnant nanny goat, lay in the center, the only one who hadn't joined the great escape. She fixed Becket with a look that seemed to say, "Don't blame me. I told them it was a bad idea."

"Well, at least one of you has some sense," Becket sighed, giving Daisy an appreciative pat. "Though I bet you would've gone too if you could have figured out a way to fit through the opening or jump the gate."

Daisy just chewed lazily, her expression now saying, "Someone's gotta be the responsible one."

Panic rising, Becket spun around, searching for his escaped herd. It didn't take long to spot them. They were scattered across the Wilson property, happily chewing on anything and everything.

The yard, which yesterday had been a wild tangle of overgrown weeds and bushes, now looked like it had been attacked by an overzealous landscaping crew armed with weed whackers and a vendetta against all things green.

"How in the world...?" Becket muttered, surveying the change. He'd thought the overgrown yard would keep his herd busy for days. Clearly, he'd underestimated their appetites. Or their ability to work as a team when properly motivated by the prospect of an all-you-can-eat buffet.

As he walked the perimeter, rounding up his now satisfied and plumper goats, Becket looked closer at the mangled remains of his makeshift fence. He could easily picture how it went down: Houdini, living up to his name, finding a weak spot and leading the great goat jailbreak.

"You sure earned your name this time, didn't you?" Becket sighed, eyeing the goat in question, who was now attempting to eat what looked like an ancient lawn gnome.

The goats hadn't caused a disaster yet, but if Becket

didn't get them back in the trailer soon, they'd be munching on the neighbor's rose bushes. He rubbed the back of his neck, scanning the yard for any escapees. With a deep breath, he stepped forward and put on his best "I'm in charge" voice.

"Alright, you four-legged freeloaders, party's over. Back to the trailer."

They just stared at him, chewing like he was the ridiculous one.

With a resigned sigh, he lunged toward the nearest goat, hoping to steer it in the right direction. That hope lasted about three seconds before the others scattered, darting around him as if playing a game. He managed to get one halfway to the trailer, only to see two more slip past him and bolt for the edge of the yard.

"Not the rosebushes!" he groaned, running after them. But it was too late.

A stubborn billy had already sunk his teeth into the shrub, yanking with enough enthusiasm to send petals flying. Becket charged over, grabbing the remains of the bush in a last-ditch tug-of-war with the goat, dirt spraying everywhere.

"Come on, you walking garbage disposals," Becket pleaded, out of breath and covered in dirt and leaves. "Work with me here!"

Just as he managed to corral half the herd into the trailer, a car approached, making Becket freeze. He turned to see a familiar Cadillac pulling up, and his heart sank. It was Marge Gunderson.

Marge stepped out of her car, her eyes widening as she took in the scene before her. Becket stood there, dirt smeared on his shirt, while a goat tugged at his sleeve, unbothered by the chaos it had caused. The yard, now trimmed of its wild overgrowth, looked mostly clean—except for the few prized rosebushes that had become a snack.

"Mr. Shepherd," Marge said, taking in the scene, "I didn't expect your goats to take their job *this* seriously."

Becket wiped a hand across his brow, trying to maintain some composure. It was tough to pull off cool when a goat was gnawing on your shirt, but he gave it his best shot. "Would you believe me if I said they're just really dedicated to their work?"

Marge held back a laugh. "Passionate, huh? I would've thought they'd know better than to touch the roses."

Becket winced, his eyes trailing to the once-beautiful rosebushes, now mostly chewed stubs. "Yeah, that was the plan. I was kind of hoping they'd stick to the weeds. Guess they've developed a taste for the finer things in life."

Marge shook her head with a sigh. "Well, despite their questionable taste in landscaping, I've got to hand it to you—this yard looks better than it has in years. Between the code enforcement office and the neighbors, I've been hearing complaints about this place for months. And here you are, getting it under control in a day."

Becket rubbed the back of his neck, relieved that Marge seemed more amused than angry. "I'll talk to them about being more discerning next time."

Marge gave him a wry look and glanced around the yard one more time.

"Speaking of next time, I have another property that could use some work. Overgrown doesn't even begin to describe it. I was just there this morning—belongs to a Ruby Whitaker. She's looking to clean it up before I can list it for her. I told her you could help."

Becket's eyebrows shot up. "You gave her my name?"

"I did," Marge confirmed. "I didn't mention your ... unique approach, but she's desperate enough that I'm sure she'll appreciate the results. Expect her to call you soon."

Becket nodded, processing the information. "Thanks for the recommendation, Marge."

She waved him off as she turned to head back to her car. "Just try to go a little easier on her flowers, okay? It'll be hard to sell a house with no landscaping left."

As Marge drove away, Becket looked down at the herd of goats, who were all staring up at him like they'd done nothing wrong.

"Alright, you hooligans," he muttered, "seems like we've got another job on the horizon. Try not to eat the entire property in one night this time."

Houdini bleated at him, as if in protest, before tugging on his shoelace.

Becket let out a sigh and managed to get the last of the goats loaded into the trailer. Just as he was about to climb into his truck, his phone rang. He glanced at the screen and answered it, half expecting Marge to have second thoughts.

"Becket Shepherd," he said, trying to sound like a guy who hadn't just spent the last hour chasing goats.

"Hi, this is Ruby Whitaker. Marge Gunderson gave me your number. She said you could help with my uncle's yard?"

Becket grinned. Well, that was quick.

"Sure thing, Ms. Whitaker. I've got a crew ready to go. When would you like me to come by?"

Ruby gave him the address and explained the state of the yard. Becket could already imagine what he was in for. Overgrown weeds, tall grass—it sounded like the perfect job for his goats.

"Tell you what," he said when she finished, "I'll swing

by this afternoon to take a look. No charge for the assessment."

After ending the call, Becket glanced back at his trailer, where the goats were peacefully munching on whatever they could find. "Alright, you gluttons, looks like we've got a chance at another gig?"

Daisy let out a bleat, and Becket chose to take it as agreement.

As he climbed into his truck and started driving toward Ruby's place, a sense of excitement surged through him. A new job and maybe a new opportunity. He just hoped Ruby wouldn't be too surprised when she saw the crew he was bringing along.

"Well, gang," he muttered, glancing in the rearview mirror at the trailer, "here's hoping Ms. Whitaker's a fan of goats."

CHAPTER SEVEN

Ruby leaned against the porch railing, tapping her foot anxiously. Flakes of old paint stuck to the soles of her shoes, evidence of how long it had been since the porch had seen a fresh coat. She'd called Becket Shepherd earlier, on Marge's recommendation, but now that he was on his way, she wasn't sure what to expect.

Marge had said he could handle the overgrown yard, but Ruby hadn't asked too many questions, too desperate to get something—anything—started.

She glanced at the yard, wincing at the sea of weeds that had once been a lawn. At this point, she half-expected to spot a family of raccoons setting up a mini subdivision out there. Maybe she could charge them property tax.

A truck engine rumbled up the drive, yanking her out of her thoughts. She straightened, instinctively sucking in her stomach—a pointless habit born from years of worrying about appearances, even though her clothes were now hanging on by a thread, quite literally. Not that anyone would notice, given they were held together with more hope than fabric. A beat-up truck rolled into view, towing a trailer that looked like it had fought through the apocalypse and lived to tell the tale.

A man hopped out, tall and broad-shouldered, dust still clinging to his jeans like he'd just walked off a construction site—or maybe stepped out of one of those home renovation shows where the host always looks impeccably rugged. Ruby waved hesitantly, trying to ignore the flutter in her stomach. Now was not the time to get distracted by a handsome face, no matter how effortlessly handsome he looked.

She'd learned her lesson after dating that smooth-talking vacuum cleaner salesman who'd left her with a top-of-the-line dust sucker and an empty wallet.

"Becket?" she called, hating how uncertain her voice sounded. It was the same tone she used when answering calls from unknown numbers, bracing for yet another debt collector.

"That's me," he replied as he sauntered toward her. His relaxed confidence made her wonder if he knew what he was in for with this yard. Either he was good at his job, or he was as clueless as a cat in a dog show.

Ruby eyed the trailer, hearing the faint sound of live animals. She wondered if she was hallucinating. Maybe the stress had gotten to her, and she was about to be carted off to a sanitarium. At least there, someone else would mow the lawn. "Uh ... what's in the trailer?"

Becket's grin widened. "The best landscaping crew you'll ever meet."

Ruby frowned, her eyebrows knitting together like two caterpillars in a wrestling match. "Landscaping crew?"

"Goats," Becket said simply, with all the confidence of a man announcing he'd discovered the secret to world peace.

She stared at him, thrown off. "You brought goats?" The words came out sharper than she intended, but seriously?

Goats? She half expected him to pull a rabbit out of his hat next and claim the rabbit was an expert in hedge trimming.

He nodded, proud of his plan. "Yep, they're efficient, eco-friendly, and love to snack on weeds. This place will be cleared out in no time."

Ruby blinked, her arms crossing instinctively. Emotions swirled within her—disbelief, frustration, and a tiny spark of curiosity. "And you expect me to pay you to let your goats eat my yard? Shouldn't you be paying me? After all, I'm feeding them." She paused, then added with a smirk, "Though I suppose I should be grateful. At least goats might be cheaper than the small army of landscapers I thought I'd need."

Becket leaned casually against his truck. The ease with which he carried himself served to heighten Ruby's agitation. Did nothing faze this guy?

"Fair point," he said. "Tell you what—we call it even. I'll clear your yard for free, and I'll just hang out while the goats get the job done."

Ruby narrowed her eyes, suspicion warring with desperation. "So, you're doing all this for free? And I just let your goats eat the yard?" She glanced at the overgrown mess. "Honestly, at this point, I'd let a herd of elephants have a go if they offered."

"Yep. Easy deal, right?" The look on Becket's face was as bold as the 'Past Due' stamps on her bills.

Ruby considered it, biting her lip. With her bank breathing down her neck and no real cash to spare, she couldn't afford to argue. Plus, free sounded good right now —a word she hadn't heard since her last sample day at the grocery store. "Fine," she relented, "but if they eat anything important, like the house or the fence, that's on you."

Becket gave a mock salute. "Deal. Don't worry, my goats

have discerning tastes. They're like the food critics of the animal world."

As he opened the trailer, Ruby held her breath. Part of her still expected this to be some elaborate prank. Maybe she was on one of those hidden camera shows. *Extreme Makeover: Bungalow Edition* or *Pimp My Yard*.

But sure enough, the goats trotted out one by one, sniffing the air like they were judging the yard's selection at a gourmet salad bar. The yard itself was bigger than most, easily spanning over half an acre, with a sturdy fence enclosing the entire property.

Ruby watched as Becket moved along the fence line, checking for any weak spots. He disappeared briefly into the edge of the woods, where the trees offered the house a good deal of privacy. After a few minutes, he circled back and headed out of the yard toward his truck.

He returned a moment later, carrying a coil of portable fencing. "I'll set this up later to keep them corralled overnight," he said, nodding toward the goats. "Even with the main fence, I like to make sure they stay in one spot after dark."

She glanced at the goats, scattered across the yard in various states of relaxation. One was nibbling lazily at a leaf; another stretched out on its side, eyes half-closed.

"So, this is what we're working with?" she asked, raising an eyebrow. "I've seen more enthusiasm from teenagers asked to clean their rooms."

Becket smirked, leaning against the fence. "They'll get to it. Goats like to take their time—wander, check things out. It's a big yard, so they'll start grazing once they're sure there's nothing dangerous around. Give them an hour, and they'll eat their way through that mess."

Becket scratched his head, watching the goats. "They're, uh ... getting acclimated."

"They look like they're on vacation," Ruby muttered, folding her arms tighter across her chest. "Maybe they think this is a resort. Should I put out some little umbrellas and coconut drinks for them?"

Becket shot her a sheepish grin. "Maybe they're unionizing. It's hard to find good help these days. Even in the goat world."

Before Ruby could respond with another quip, her phone buzzed in her pocket. She glanced at the screen and groaned. The bank. Again. It was like they had a sixth sense for when she was starting to feel a glimmer of hope.

With a deep breath, she answered quietly, turning away from Becket. "Yes, I'm aware the payment is overdue. I'll take care of it as soon as I can." She paused, listening to the stern voice on the other end. "No, I don't need another reminder, thank you." She hung up, trying to shove down the wave of frustration as she turned back to Becket, who was watching her curiously.

"Everything okay?" he asked, his tone casual, but there was something knowing in his eyes that made Ruby feel exposed. Great, now the handsome goat-herder knew she was one step away from having to give serious consideration to the house's resale value.

Ruby waved it off, but the words slipped out anyway, tinged with bitterness. "Just my bank reminding me I'm broke. Funny, I was planning on using my credit card to pay you, but now I guess I don't have to." She forced a laugh. "Silver linings, right? Though at this point, I'd settle for copper linings. Or tin. Really, any metal that isn't worthless."

Becket's lips twitched in amusement. "Seems like I'm saving you more than just a landscaping bill, huh?"

Ruby huffed, embarrassment and gratitude coloring her cheeks. "Guess so. You sure this is going to work? The goats look less interested in the yard than I am." She nodded towards one goat who seemed to be admiring itself in the reflection of an old, rusted hubcap. "That one looks like he's posing for his LinkedIn profile picture."

"They'll get going," Becket said with a grin that was far too infectious for Ruby's liking. "They're just sizing up the place. Once they start, they'll be like furry lawnmowers."

Ruby rolled her eyes, fighting the amusement threatening to show.

There was something about Becket's easy-going nature that made her want to believe him, despite the ridiculousness of the situation. "Well, they better get moving soon. This yard isn't going to fix itself." The lightness in her tone surprised her.

Becket gave a playful nod. "Trust me, once they're done, you won't even recognize this place. And if they don't ... well, I've got a backup plan."

Ruby raised an eyebrow, curiosity piqued. "What's the backup plan? A herd of sheep with weed-whackers strapped to their backs?"

"Close," Becket grinned. "I've got an old lawnmower in the back of my truck. But I'm sure they'll get to work before I need it. These goats are professionals. They just ... take their time."

Just as he said that, one of the goats bent down and took a small, experimental nibble of a weed. Ruby watched, holding her breath. But then, the goat promptly walked away, disinterested, like a food critic dismissing an appetizer.

Becket sighed, rubbing the back of his neck. "Okay, maybe they're on a break. Union rules, you know."

Ruby let out a short laugh, surprising herself. "Some landscapers."

As they stood there, watching the goats meander about, a strange mix of emotions welled up in Ruby. On one hand, the pressure of her financial situation loomed large, threatening to crush her spirits. On the other, there was something almost ... liberating about the absurdity of it all. Here she was, pinning her hopes on a bunch of goats and a man who looked more like he belonged on a home improvement show than in her overgrown yard.

She glanced at Becket, noticing his eyes still on her as he watched quietly.

Their eyes met, and something sparked to life inside her.

It was something that made her forget about the bank calls and the mounting bills, even if just for a second. It reminded her of being back in high school, catching her crush's eye across the cafeteria. Except now, instead of a cafeteria, they stood in a weedy wasteland, and instead of fellow students, they were surrounded by unhurried goats.

"You know," Becket said, breaking the silence, "I have a feeling these goats are going to surprise us both."

She paused, then said, "If this doesn't work out, maybe we can start a petting zoo. Come see the world's laziest goats and the woman who thought they'd save her inherited bungalow!"

As if on cue, one of the goats took a big bite of the overgrown grass. Ruby and Becket exchanged a look of triumphant amusement.

"See?" Becket grinned. "Told you they'd come through. They just needed a dramatic moment."

And as Ruby watched the goat continue to munch, hope settled in. Things were starting to look up. Even if it took a herd of reluctant goats and a far-too-charming landscaper to make it happen.

"Alright," she said, straightening up. "While your crew gets to work, why don't you tell me more about this grand plan of yours? And maybe explain why you decided that goat herding was a natural progression from landscaping. I could use a good laugh."

Becket's eyes twinkled with amusement. "Oh, it's a long story. Involves a mistaken Craigslist ad and a mid-day epiphany. But I warn you, it might just convince you that I'm either a genius or insane."

Ruby let out a laugh, surprising herself with how genuine it was. "Well, Becket, I'm currently watching a goat treat my overgrown lawn like an all-you-can-eat buffet. I think I left 'normal' behind a long time ago." She gestured towards the porch. "Come on, I might even have some lemonade that hasn't expired yet. We can watch your crew work, and you can tell me all about your journey from landscaper to goat whisperer."

As they walked toward the porch, a sense of lightness settled over Ruby, one she hadn't experienced in months. Sure, her problems were far from solved. The bank wasn't going to stop calling just because she had a handsome man and his herd of goats in her yard. But for the first time in a long while, she thought that she could face those problems head-on.

And who knew? If Becket's crazy idea worked, she might just have to rethink her stance on unconventional solutions. After all, in a world where goats could be landscapers, anything was possible.

CHAPTER EIGHT

Becket awoke to goats bleating and the first light of dawn filtering through the worn canvas of his tent. He blinked away the remnants of sleep, momentarily disoriented by the unfamiliar surroundings. Then it all came rushing back—Ruby's overgrown yard, his landscaping offer, and the makeshift camp he'd set up for himself and his goats. He glanced toward the nearby trees, where he and the goats were probably the only ones keeping the woods hydrated.

With a groan, he unzipped the tent flap and stepped out into the cool morning air of Ruby's backyard. The goats were already up, bleating impatiently, eager to resume their feast from yesterday. The yard, which had seemed like an insurmountable jungle when they'd first arrived, was starting to show signs of progress. Patches of neatly trimmed grass peeked out amidst the remaining overgrowth, like islands of order in a sea of chaos.

"Morning, gang," Becket said, as he made his way to the makeshift pen. "Ready for another day of five-star dining?"

As if in response, Houdini let out an enthusiastic bleat. Of all his goats, Houdini seemed to be enjoying this landscaping gig the most. The goat had a glint in his eye that seemed to say, "All this food, and we're not even in trouble for eating it? Best job ever!"

The back door of Ruby's house creaked open, drawing Becket's attention. He turned to see Ruby step out onto the porch, and his breath caught in his throat. Even with her hair pulled back in a messy bun and wearing what looked like old paint-splattered overalls, she was a sight for sore eyes. She balanced two steaming mugs in her hands, navigating the porch steps with careful determination.

"Morning, Goat Whisperer," she called out, her voice still a bit groggy but tinged with amusement. "Did you sleep okay? I thought you might need this." She held out one of the mugs. "It's strong enough to wake the dead, or at least strong enough to deal with a herd of hungry goats."

Becket's eyes lit up like a kid on Christmas morning. "Coffee? You're an angel," he said, reaching for the mug with both hands as if it were the Holy Grail. He took a long sip and let out a contented sigh that was almost comical in its exaggeration. "Oh, sweet caffeine, how I've missed you."

Ruby watched his theatrics with amusement. "Wow, if I'd known coffee would get that kind of reaction, I'd have led with it yesterday. Should I leave you two alone?"

Becket grinned over the rim of his mug. "Hey, don't judge. When you're living the glamorous life of a goat landscaper, good coffee is harder to come by than you'd think. Last week, I was so desperate I tried to convince myself that chewing on coffee grounds was just as good."

"And how did that work out for you?" Ruby asked, raising an eyebrow.

"Let's just say the goats were not impressed with my breath," Becket replied with a wink. "This, though? This is heaven. You may have just saved lives with this coffee, Ruby. The goats thank you."

As if on cue, one of the goats let out a loud bleat.

"See?" Becket said, gesturing towards the goat with his mug. "Daisy agrees."

Ruby laughed, shaking her head. "Well, I'm glad I could contribute to the cause. Just don't let it go to your head, Goat Whisperer. I expect those landscapers of yours to work extra hard today, caffeinated or not."

"Yes, ma'am," Becket said, taking another long sip of coffee. "With this fuel, we'll have your yard looking like a golf course by sundown."

As they stood there, sipping their coffee and watching the goats begin their day's work, a sense of contentment washed over Becket. It was a feeling he hadn't experienced in a long time, not since losing his farm. He snuck a glance at Ruby, wondering if she felt it too—this strange sense of rightness, as though the universe had clicked into place.

"So," Ruby said, breaking the comfortable silence, "what's on the agenda for today? More strategic goat placement? Or are we moving on to advanced techniques like synchronized grazing?"

Becket appreciated her newfound enthusiasm for his methods. "Well, I was thinking we'd start with a rousing game of 'Pin the Goat on the Weed,' followed by an intense session of 'Extreme Munching.' You know, push the boundaries of landscaping innovation."

Ruby snorted into her coffee. "Oh, of course. How silly of me to think it would be anything less than revolutionary."

As the morning wore on, Becket guided his goats through the yard, focusing on the areas they'd missed the day before. The sun climbed higher in the sky, beating down relentlessly and turning the air thick and humid.

Becket wiped the sweat from his brow, grateful for the caffeine boost that was keeping him going.

Ruby alternated between watching from the porch and disappearing into the house to tackle her own mountain of indoor tasks. Each time she emerged, Becket straightened up a little, attempting to look more professional than he was. It was silly. He was covered in sweat and bits of grass, surrounded by stinky goats. Professional wasn't in the cards.

"How's it going, Goat Whisperer?" Ruby called out during one of her check-ins, a smirk playing at the corners of her mouth.

Becket grinned, wiping his hands on his jeans. "Oh, you know, just living the dream. Nothing like spending a beautiful day watching grass ... disappear."

Just as he was about to elaborate on the joys of goats, a loud crash from behind made them both jump. Becket whirled around to see Daisy looking sheepishly at the remains of what appeared to be an old garden statue.

"Oh no," Ruby groaned, her hand flying to her mouth.

Becket's heart sank. This was it. The moment when Ruby would realize that letting a herd of goats loose in her yard might not have been the best idea. He rushed over to assess the damage, apologies already forming on his lips.

"I am so sorry," he said, crouching down next to the broken statue. It had once been ... well, he wasn't quite sure. A cherub, maybe? Or perhaps a chubby fairy? Now, tacky porcelain shards littered the overgrown grass. Daisy stood nearby, chewing nonchalantly as if she hadn't just committed an act of garden vandalism.

To Becket's utter surprise, Ruby burst out laughing—full-bodied, doubled-over laughter that seemed to bubble up from her soul. "Oh my god," she wheezed between gales of laughter. "Did you see her face? She looked so guilty!"

Becket blinked, relief washing over him. "So ... you're not mad?"

Ruby shook her head, still fighting to catch her breath. "Are you kidding? That thing was hideous. My uncle must have picked it up at a yard sale. Now I don't have to figure out how to get rid of it without feeling guilty."

As Ruby's laughter subsided, Becket joined in. The absurdity of the situation—a goat solving Ruby's dilemma—was too much to resist. They stood there, laughing together in the middle of the overgrown yard.

When they caught their breath, Ruby wiped a tear from her eye. "You know, Becket, when Marge gave me your number, I wasn't sure what to expect. But I have to admit, this is the most fun I've had in ... well, longer than I can remember."

Becket's chest tightened in a way that had nothing to do with the summer heat. "I aim to please. Landscaping and entertainment, all in one package."

Ruby's expression softened, the tension lifting from her face as her eyes crinkled at the corners. It was a nice change from the worried frown she'd worn when he first arrived.

As they settled on the porch steps, Becket relaxed for the first time in weeks. The goats continued their work in the background, providing a strangely soothing soundtrack of munching and occasional bleats. He made a mental note to clean up the shards of the broken statue later—goats weren't exactly picky, and he didn't want them mistaking them for a snack.

"So," Ruby said, taking a sip of her drink, "how does a guy end up in the goat landscaping business anyway? I'm guessing it wasn't your childhood dream."

Becket's expression softened, though a hint of sadness lingered in his eyes. "No. This is a new gig. I had a farm, not too far from here. Goat farm, if you can believe it. We made cheese, milk, the whole nine yards."

"Wow." Ruby's eyebrows shot up. "What happened?"

Becket sighed, running a hand through his hair. "Drought hit. Hit hard. Feed prices went through the roof, and then the land I was renting got sold out from under me. Before I knew it, I was scrambling to keep my herd fed and housed."

Ruby's face softened, understanding dawning in her eyes. "That must have been tough."

"Yeah," Becket nodded, his gaze distant. "I had to sell most of the herd. Couldn't bear to part with all of them, though. These guys," he gestured to the goats in the yard, "they're like family. So, I had to get creative."

"And that's how you ended up in landscaping?"

Becket nodded thoughtfully. "I was looking for a spot for the goats to graze and came across a vacant home. The yard was overrun with weeds, so I contacted the listing agent, Marge Gunderson, to see if we could work something out. One thing led to another, and now I've got a whole side gig. It's a new thing."

Ruby laughed. "A whole business, just like that?"

"Yeah, pretty much," Becket said, grinning. "It just sort of fell into place."

Ruby shook her head in disbelief. "That's ... kind of brilliant. In a crazy way."

"Hey, sometimes crazy is all we've got," Becket shrugged.

They fell into a comfortable silence, watching the goats work. Becket snuck a glance at Ruby, noticing how the tension she'd been carrying in her shoulders seemed to have eased a bit.

"What about you?" he asked. "How'd you end up here?"

Ruby sighed, twirling her glass in her hands. "Inherited the place from my uncle. I was struggling in Chicago, free-lancing and just scraping by. Then, I get this letter saying I've got a house in Aspen Cove. Seemed like a lifeline, you know?"

Becket nodded, understanding all too well how desperation can lead to grasping at any opportunity when things got tough.

"But now," Ruby continued, her voice tinged with frustration, "I'm here, and it's … overwhelming. The house is a mess, the yard was a jungle until you showed up, and I've got the bank breathing down my neck about credit card payments I can hardly afford."

"Starting over is never easy," Becket said.

Ruby tilted her head, studying his face. "Is that what this is for you? Starting over?"

Becket nodded. "Every day. It's a strange mix of terrifying and exhilarating."

"I know the feeling," Ruby said, glancing at the goats as they continued their feast.

As the hours passed, they shared stories about the unexpected turns life took, their dreams, and the fears that came with starting anew. The sun climbed higher, and Ruby's stomach growled, interrupting their conversation.

"Looks like that coffee wasn't enough to get us through the day," Ruby said, laughing. "I'll try to find something we can eat in the kitchen. It's the least I can do for all this."

Becket nodded. "That sounds good."

Ruby headed back into the house, leaving Becket to finish corralling the last of the goats. His stomach grumbled, reminding him that it had been hours since he had eaten. He wondered what she might dig up from that old kitchen.

A few minutes later, Ruby returned holding two mismatched plates with a spread that was, at best, questionable. "So, here's what I've got—a little peanut butter with crackers. I found some tuna, too, but I wouldn't recommend it unless you're up for mystery flavors. One can had corn and carrots mixed in."

Becket took the plate, chuckling. "Honestly, this beats half the meals I've had on the road."

Ruby plopped down beside him on the porch steps. "Just giving you fair warning, though—no idea how old the peanut butter is, so ... eat at your own risk."

He took a bite. "I've survived worse."

They ate in silence, but then a breeze swept through, and Becket shivered as the distinct chill of winter crept in. He glanced up at the sky, noticing how it was darkening. "Feels like the weather's turning."

Ruby hugged herself against the wind. "Yeah, I was thinking that, too. Do your goats have enough shelter if it gets colder tonight?"

Becket looked over at the herd, now huddled together, content after a long day of grazing. "They'll be alright for now, but if it drops much lower, I'll have to think about something better than what they've got."

Ruby looked at him with a hint of concern. "And what about you? That tent doesn't scream 'warm and cozy.'"

He shrugged, finishing his last cracker. "It's not ideal, but the truck cab's a lot warmer than the tent. I've slept in there plenty of times when it gets too cold."

Ruby glanced at the near-empty plate between them. "Well, I'm not sure this gourmet meal will keep you warm, but at least you won't be hungry tonight."

He wiped his hands. "It's not half bad, especially since I didn't have to cook it."

She stood up, brushing off her hands. "Neither did I. And it was free, which is just about all I can afford right now."

They both stood, the air now heavy with the promise of a chillier night ahead. Becket glanced at the yard—still a work in progress, but undeniably better than when he first arrived.

"Tomorrow, we'll finish clearing the weeds out," Becket said, rubbing the back of his neck. "We're making good progress, but there's still work to do."

Ruby nodded, glancing around. "You know, your goat method is kind of growing on me."

He nodded as he gathered his things. "I'll see you in the morning."

"Bright and early," Ruby replied, teasing. "Just don't freeze in that tent of yours, okay?"

Becket flashed a grin. "I'll survive," he said, giving her a nod before turning and heading back toward the edge of the yard where his tent was pitched.

Once inside, he unzipped the flap and ducked in. The cold night air crept in with him, but he ignored it as he settled into his sleeping bag. With a sigh, he lay back, staring up at the tent's canvas roof. But instead of closing his eyes, he found himself leaning over and peeking out of the tent flap. From his spot in the trees, he could just make out Ruby's house in the distance. She was planning to sell it, but after a day like today, part of him hoped she'd stick around a little longer.

CHAPTER NINE

Ruby woke with the first light of dawn, her mind already racing with plans for the day ahead. The events of yesterday played through her mind—Becket's easy laughter, the way he'd looked at her over his coffee mug, the surprising fun of watching goats demolish her yard. She shook off the warm, fuzzy feeling that threatened to take root. This was temporary, she reminded herself. Clean up, sell, get out. That was the plan.

Still, as she padded to the kitchen in her worn slippers, a twinge of ... something settled in her chest. Anticipation, maybe? Or just indigestion from yesterday's questionable peanut butter?

The fridge greeted her with its usual barren landscape. Ruby sighed, eyeing the lone occupant—a block of cheese that had somehow managed to grow greener than the entire yard. She closed the door, half-afraid the cheese might sprout legs and walk away on its own.

"Alright, Rubes," she muttered to herself, "time to get creative. Goat Whisperer out there deserves better than stale crackers two days in a row."

After some rummaging through the pantry, Ruby emerged victorious with her spoils: a can of baked beans and a tin of Spam that looked like it might have survived a nuclear apocalypse.

Determined to make the best of it, Ruby set about cooking their meager feast. She dumped the beans into a pot, stirring them as they heated on the ancient stove. The Spam she sliced and tossed into a pan, where it sizzled and filled the kitchen with a scent that was equal parts nostalgic and concerning.

Ruby laughed to herself as she plated up her culinary masterpiece, struck by the absurdity of it all. She peered out the kitchen window, searching for signs of life in the yard. Becket's tent was still zipped up, but she noticed movement inside. The goats were in their temporary pen at the far end of the yard, near where the grass gave way to scattered trees.

"Hope you're ready for a real treat, Becket," she called out as she headed to the porch, balancing two plates. "We're having a five-star breakfast of beans à la tin and artisanal preserved meat product!"

She set the plates down on the small porch table and settled into a chair, scanning the yard. Just as she was about to take a bite, Becket emerged from his tent, stretching and running a hand through his tousled hair.

"Morning, Ruby!" he called out, his joy visible even from a distance. "Wow, breakfast service too? You're spoiling me." He glanced at the goat pen and then back at Ruby with a grin. "Give me two minutes to let these guys out, and I'll join you."

Ruby watched, amused, as Becket made his way to the goat pen. As soon as he unlatched the gate, the goats eagerly pushed their way out, spreading across the yard with enthusiasm. One exuberant goat pranced around Becket, bleating happily.

"You know," Becket called out between laughs as he made sure all the goats were out, "I think these guys are more excited about their breakfast than we are about ours!"

True to his word, he was soon bounding up the porch steps, out of breath but still smiling. His eyes twinkled with amusement as he took in the breakfast spread.

"Well, this looks … interesting," he said, settling into the chair across from her. "I appreciate the effort. Beats my usual granola bar on the go."

As they ate, Ruby relaxed into easy conversation with Becket. There was something comforting about his presence, a steadiness that made her feel grounded despite the chaos of her current situation. They watched the goats grazing in the yard, some venturing toward the edge of the wooded area, which sat within the fenced property, in search of tasty leaves and shrubs.

The day passed in a blur of dust and discoveries. Ruby unearthed more of Uncle Peter's eclectic collection—vintage cameras that looked like they belonged in a museum, a box full of novelty shot glasses from every state, including ones Uncle Peter had definitely never visited, and enough books to stock a small library.

Every so often, she'd peek out the window, catching glimpses of Becket as he kept an eye on the goats, occasionally straightening a patch of fencing or clearing debris. Once, she could have sworn she saw him doing a little dance with one of the goats near the edge of the wooded area, twirling it around like a furry dance partner. The sight made her laugh out loud, a sound that seemed foreign in the quiet house.

As the afternoon wore on, Ruby took more and more

breaks to chat with Becket. She told him about her life in Chicago, the soul-crushing corporate job she'd left behind, and the freelance career that had promised freedom but delivered mostly stress and unpaid invoices.

A knock at the door broke Ruby's focus. She got up and opened it to find Becket standing there, water bottle in hand.

"Mind if I refill this?" he asked, nodding toward the kitchen.

"You don't have to ask, you can just come in," she said, stepping aside to let him through.

He smiled and headed for the sink. "Thanks," he said, as he refilled the bottle and glanced out the window at the goats. Ruby returned to the kitchen table, her fingers moving through the clutter in the open box.

Her hand brushed against something cool and smooth. "What's this?" she muttered, pulling out an old mason jar. Her eyes widened as she unscrewed the lid and poured out the contents. Coins clattered onto the floor, along with a few crumpled bills.

"Well, would you look at that," Becket said, glancing over as he screwed the cap back onto his bottle. "Looks like your uncle left you a little treasure after all."

Ruby counted, her heart racing. It wasn't a fortune by any means, but it was enough for a decent grocery run. Maybe even a nice dinner out. She looked up at Becket, excitement dancing in her eyes. "Hey, what do you say we treat ourselves to dinner in town? I heard there's a place called Maisey's that's supposed to be good."

Becket's eyebrows shot up. "Are you sure? I mean, you don't have to—"

"I'm not," Ruby interrupted with a grin. "Uncle Peter is.

Come on, it'll be fun. Plus, I could use a break from all this dust."

Before they left, Ruby and Becket stepped outside to check on the goats. The animals grazed, content and unaware of the world beyond the fence.

"They should be fine," Becket said, giving the fence a once-over. "I'll check on them when we get back."

Satisfied, they walked into town. Twenty minutes later, they entered Maisey's Diner. The bell above the door jingled as they stepped inside, and the aroma of coffee and home-cooked food filled the air. The diner looked like it hadn't changed much since the 1950s, with its red vinyl booths and chrome-edged tables. A few heads turned to look at the newcomers, curiosity in their gazes.

A thin woman with a neatly styled bob approached them, wiping her hands on an apron tied snugly around her waist. Her eyes sparkled as she spoke.

"Well, hello there! Don't think I've seen you two around before. I'm Maisey, and this here's my place. What brings you to Aspen Cove?"

"Hi, I'm Ruby Whitaker," she said. "I inherited my Uncle Peter's house—"

"Peter Larkin's niece!" Maisey exclaimed, her face lighting up. "Well, I'll be! Your uncle was a regular here. It's so good to meet you, honey." She turned to Becket.

"Becket Shepherd," he introduced himself with a nod. "I'm helping Ruby with some landscaping."

"With goats," Ruby added, unable to keep the amusement out of her voice.

Maisey's eyes widened. "Goats? Well, now that's a story I've got to hear. Come on in, let's get you two settled. I hope you're ready for some real food. Can't have you wasting away on whatever's left in that old house of Peter's." She grabbed two menus from behind the counter. "Before we get to that goat tale, how about I set you up with our blue plate special? It's meatloaf tonight."

Ruby and Becket exchanged glances. "Sounds great," Ruby said, speaking for both of them.

"Perfect! Two blue plates coming right up," Maisey said as she led them to a booth. Ruby noticed the other patrons watching with interest. In Aspen Cove, it seemed that news of a new face spread fast.

Once they sat down, Maisey asked, "What can I get you to drink?"

"I'll have a coffee," Becket said, glancing at Ruby.

"Same for me," Ruby added.

Maisey nodded. "Coming right up."

A few minutes later, Maisey returned with two steaming cups of coffee. "Here you go. Food will be out soon."

They sipped their drinks, chatting about the town. Not long after, Maisey appeared again, skillfully balancing two plates. She set them down with a flourish, proudly declaring, "The best damn meatloaf this side of the Rockies. Enjoy, you two!"

Ruby inhaled deeply, the savory aroma making her mouth water. She was about to dig in when a cheerful woman approached their table with a wave.

"Hi, I'm Katie! I own B's Bakery across the street. You should stop by sometime—first treat is on me," she said. Next to her stood a tall man with an easygoing grin, holding the hand of a little girl who was clinging to his leg.

"This is my husband, Bowie, and our daughter, Sahara," Katie added. Sahara, about five years old, peeked out shyly before grinning up at Ruby.

"Nice to meet you," Ruby said, warmed by the family's kindheartedness.

As they settled in, a few other townspeople wandered over to introduce themselves, each offering a friendly word or invitation. Even Sheriff Aiden Cooper, who had been sitting across the room, stopped by to shake Ruby and Becket's hands.

By the time they started eating, Ruby's nerves had eased. The food was delicious, the company lively, and the whole diner gave the impression of a tight-knit community welcoming her in. Even the scratchy old country tunes from the jukebox added to the cozy appeal of the place.

After dinner, Ruby insisted they stop by the Corner Store. "We can't keep living on canned beans and Spam," she told Becket as they perused the aisles. "Besides, I think that cheese in the fridge is plotting a takeover. I swear I heard it muttering 'vive la revolution' this morning."

Becket laughed. The sound made Ruby's heart do a little flip. "Well, we can't have a cheese uprising on our hands. That would be an embarrassing way to lose control of the house."

They left the store laden with bags full of staples—bread, eggs, milk, and enough fresh produce to make Ruby feel like she was back in civilization. As they walked back to the house under a sky full of stars, Ruby stole glances at Becket. In the soft glow of the streetlights, he looked ... different. Softer, somehow. More real.

"Thanks for coming with me tonight," Ruby said as they reached the front porch. "It was nice to get out of the house for a bit."

Becket smiled, and that now-familiar flutter stirred in Ruby's stomach. "Thanks for inviting me. It was fun getting to know the town a little better."

They stood together, the cool evening air settling around them. Becket glanced toward the backyard, then back at Ruby. "I should check on the goats before it gets too late. They tend to get a bit adventurous in the evenings, with all those trees tempting them."

Ruby nodded, watching as he walked away into the night, his figure gradually disappearing into the shadows cast by the trees at the far end of the yard. There was something steady and reassuring about him, like the town itself—a quiet strength that was beginning to grow on her.

As Ruby got ready for bed that night, her mind buzzed with the day's whirlwind. The house still seemed like a mountain to climb, but now there was a glimmer of possibility in every cluttered corner. And Aspen Cove ... maybe it wasn't quite the backwater she'd pegged it for. There was something irresistible about the town, a tight-knit community that felt worlds apart from her life in Chicago.

She picked up the photo of Uncle Peter she'd found earlier, studying his smiling face. "Okay, Uncle Peter," she said. "I'm starting to see why you loved this place. What else do you have to show me?"

CHAPTER TEN

The usual chorus of bleating that served as his alarm clock was conspicuously absent. Becket blinked, rubbing the sleep from his eyes, and peeked out of his tent. A thin blanket of snow covered the ground, transforming Ruby's yard into a winter wonderland.

"Well, I'll be," he muttered, a grin spreading across his face. "Looks like winter decided to show up. Just in time for Christmas."

His moment of awe was short-lived as he noticed something else: the makeshift pen where his goats should have been was scattered in pieces and he could make out a few hoof prints in the fresh snow. Only Daisy, his heavily pregnant goat, remained, standing still and staring pointedly toward the back fence, as if telling on her more nimble companions.

"Oh no," Becket groaned, scrambling out of the tent. "No, no, no. This can't be happening."

He hurried over to the pen and did a quick headcount. A few of the goats were wandering around the yard, nosing through the snow, but as Becket counted again, his stomach sank—one goat was missing.

"Not again," he muttered, his eyes following Daisy's accusatory gaze toward the back fence.

That's when he spotted it—hoof prints leading to an old barrel he hadn't noticed before, sitting right next to the fence.

"Houdini," Becket groaned. "Of course."

It was obvious what had happened. The naughty goat had used the barrel to clear the fence, leaving Daisy behind to keep watch. Becket sighed, pulling on his boots and bracing himself for the inevitable chase. The tracks disappeared into the snowy landscape beyond the yard.

Without wasting another moment, Becket sprinted towards Ruby's house, his boots crunching in the snow. He bounded up the porch steps two at a time and knocked on the door with more force than he intended.

A bleary-eyed Ruby answered, her hair a messy nest and her oversized sweater hanging off one shoulder. "Becket? What's wrong? It's not even dawn."

"Houdini's gone," Becket blurted. "I need your help to find him before he gets into trouble."

Ruby's eyes widened, suddenly alert. "Gone? How? When?"

"Must've been during the night," Becket explained, gesturing to the snowy landscape. "The snow covered his tracks. He could be anywhere by now."

Ruby bit her lip, worry etching lines across her forehead. "Okay, let me grab my coat. We'll find him."

As Ruby hurried to get ready, a wave of gratitude washed over Becket. Here she was, jumping into action without hesitation, even though she hardly knew him or his goats.

"Hey," Ruby said, reappearing at the door, bundled up in a winter coat. "Alright, Goat Whisperer. Let's go find your escape artist."

They set out into the chilly morning, their breath forming little clouds in the air. As they walked towards town, Ruby's anxiety seemed to grow.

"What if we don't find him?" she asked. "What if he's hurt? Or worse, what if he's destroying someone's property? Oh god, everyone's going to hate me. I'm the newcomer who let a destructive goat loose in their town."

Becket placed a reassuring hand on her shoulder. "Hey, don't worry. Houdini's smart. He's just looking for a good meal."

Ruby didn't look convinced, but she nodded, squaring her shoulders as they entered the main street.

It didn't take long to spot the trail of destruction. A string of half-eaten garlands led them down the sidewalk.

"Oh no," Ruby groaned. "This is a disaster."

They rounded the corner to find Houdini standing triumphantly atop a pyramid of Christmas presents that had been part of the town's holiday display. The goat was munching on a cardboard star, tinsel draped across his horns like a festive boa.

"Houdini!" Becket yelled. "Get down from there, you troublemaker!"

The goat looked up, regarding them with what could be described as a smug expression. Then, with the agility of a much smaller animal, he leapt from the display and took off down the street.

What followed was a chase through town. Becket and Ruby slipped and slid on icy patches, got tangled in fallen decorations, and apologized profusely to every person they encountered.

"I'm so sorry," Ruby panted to Katie as they raced past B's Bakery. "I promise I'll replace everything!"

Katie, standing in the doorway with a tray of fresh muffins, just laughed. "Don't worry, honey. This is the most excitement we've had since Old Man Jenkins tried to convince everyone he'd seen Bigfoot in his backyard!"

As they turned into Hope Park, they found Houdini engaged in a standoff with Sheriff Cooper. The goat was eyeing the tinsel on the gazebo, while Aiden was trying to lure him with his half-eaten muffin.

"Houdini, no!" Becket called out, just as the goat made a leap for the gazebo.

In a move that would have made any action movie proud, Becket dove forward, arms outstretched. He managed to grab Houdini mid-jump, both of them tumbling onto the ground.

"Gotcha!" Becket yelled.

Ruby rushed over. "Are you okay?"

Becket grinned up at her, snow clinging to his hair and Houdini tucked firmly under his arm. "Never better." He looked down at the goat. "I'm telling you, Houdini, one more stunt like this and you might find yourself the main ingredient in a goat stew. How does that sound, you tinsel-eating troublemaker?"

Houdini, for his part, merely bleated, seeming entirely unperturbed by the threat or his recent misadventures.

Ruby laughed at the pair of them. "I don't know, Becket. Looks to me like he's proud of himself. Might even be planning his next great escape."

Becket groaned. "Don't give him any ideas. Next thing you know, he'll be leaving ransom notes made of chewed-up garland."

Ruby laughed, her eyes crinkling with amusement. Becket could imagine how ridiculous he must look, covered in snow and tinsel, clutching a disgruntled goat.

As they stood up, brushing off snow and bits of decoration, Sheriff Cooper approached, shaking his head.

"Well, folks," he said, "I'd say this qualifies as disturbing the peace, but I'm not sure our town bylaws cover renegade goats."

Ruby's face fell, the humor of the moment evaporating. "I'm so sorry, Sheriff. This is all my fault. I'll pay for any damages and—"

Aiden held up a hand to cut her off, a hint of amusement in his voice. "Relax. No harm done. Haven't seen this many people out and about since the big Christmas tree burned down last year."

As if to prove his point, townspeople continued to emerge from their homes and shops, drawn by the excitement. Soon, a small crowd had gathered, all chattering and laughing about Houdini's adventures.

Ruby looked around in amazement. Instead of the anger and resentment she'd feared, she was met with friendly smiles and easy laughter.

Becket's hand settled on her shoulder, and she turned to find him smiling, though a hint of surprise lingered in his eyes.

"Well, I'll be damned," he said. "I thought for sure Houdini would get us both into trouble."

"I know," Ruby said, her guilt weighing on her. "But look at all this damage," she added, gesturing to the chewed decorations and toppled displays. "I have to make this right."

Becket squeezed her shoulder. "We'll figure it out. I'm

as surprised as you are but looks like they're not holding a grudge. Don't worry."

"I'll replace everything," she announced, her voice carrying over the chatter of the crowd. "All the decorations, the displays, everything. I promise."

The townspeople turned to look at her, surprise evident on their faces.

"Oh, honey," Maisey said, her voice gentle. "You don't have to do that. It's just a bit of tinsel and cardboard."

"But I want to," Ruby insisted. "It's the least I can do after all this trouble."

Becket watched her, a mix of admiration and concern deep in his eyes. He knew she didn't have the means to follow through on her promise, but he couldn't help admiring her determination to make things right.

As the crowd dispersed, Ruby turned to Becket, her eyes blazing with determination and frustration. "How could you let this happen?" she demanded. "I thought you had these goats under control!"

Becket's eyebrows shot up. "Let this happen? Ruby, goats aren't known for their obedience. Houdini's always been a handful."

"Then maybe you shouldn't have brought him!" she shot back. "Do you have any idea how this makes me look? I'm trying to fit in here, and now I'm the girl who let a destructive goat loose in town!"

Becket's face hardened. "I didn't plan for this, you know. And may I remind you, you're the one who agreed to let me bring the goats in the first place."

They glared at each other, the tension palpable. Then, as quickly as it had flared up, the anger drained away, leaving them both looking tired and a bit sheepish.

"I'm sorry," Ruby said. "I know it's not your fault. I'm just … I'm overwhelmed."

Becket's expression softened. "I know. I'm sorry too. I should have been more careful with Houdini. We'll figure this out, okay?"

Ruby nodded, offering him a small smile. "Okay."

As they walked back toward Ruby's house, Houdini securely leashed this time, Ruby's mind was clearly working on a plan. She'd go through Uncle Peter's belongings, see if there was anything valuable that she could sell to fund the replacement decorations. It was a long shot, but it was all she had.

"You know," Becket said as they approached the house, "I think you might have underestimated this town. They seem to like you, goat chaos and all."

Ruby paused, feeling a sense of contentment wash over her. "Yeah, I'm starting to think I might have underestimated a lot of things about Aspen Cove."

As they reached the porch, Ruby turned to Becket. "Listen, why don't you come in for a bit? You must be freezing after all that. I can make us some coffee, and we can start figuring out how to goat-proof the yard."

Becket hesitated, glancing back at his truck. "I should get the other goats settled…"

"Come on," Ruby insisted. "Just for a little while. Consider it my way of saying sorry for snapping at you earlier."

"Alright," Becket nodded. "Just for a bit. But let me get this guy locked up first." He turned to Houdini, who was eyeing him with what looked suspiciously like amusement. "Come on, you troublemaker. Time for a timeout."

A few minutes later, Becket stepped into the house, shaking off snow and removing his damp coat. Something had shifted. This morning's chaos had been unexpected, embarrassing, and more than a little stressful. But as he watched Ruby in the kitchen making coffee, he had the sense that he might be exactly where he was supposed to be. Glancing out the window at Houdini in his pen, a fond exasperation on his face, Becket looked forward to whatever adventure this strange little town might throw at them next.

CHAPTER ELEVEN

Ruby wiped sweat from her brow as she hauled another box down from the attic. She'd been at it for hours, sorting through Uncle Peter's belongings in a desperate search for anything valuable. The events of yesterday—Houdini's escape, the destruction of the town's Christmas decorations, and her impulsive promise to make everything right— weighed heavily on her mind.

"Way to go, Ruby," she muttered, setting the box down with a thud. "Promise to replace everything when you can't even afford to feed yourself. Brilliant plan."

Pausing to catch her breath, Ruby shuffled to the window. The world outside was blanketed in white, the season transforming Aspen Cove into a winter wonderland. In the yard, she could see Becket already up and about, tending to his goats. Even from a distance, she could tell he was giving Houdini a stern talking-to.

The sight almost made her laugh. Despite the chaos that he had caused, there was something oddly endearing about that troublemaking goat. And as for Becket ... Ruby pushed that thought aside. She had more pressing matters to deal with.

"Alright, Uncle Peter," she said, turning to survey the cluttered room. "Time to see if you left me anything worth selling."

Over the next few hours, Ruby dove headfirst into sorting through her uncle's things. She started in the attic, working her way down, uncovering years of accumulated ... well, junk. There was no other way to put it. Uncle Peter had been a collector of the strange, the useless, and the outright bizarre.

In one dusty corner of the attic, she found a collection of souvenir spoons from places he'd never been. "Really, Uncle Peter?" Ruby muttered, holding up a spoon engraved with 'I ♥ North Korea.' "I'm pretty sure you never set foot in Pyongyang."

Moving to the bedroom, she discovered a box filled with pairs of mismatched socks, each meticulously labeled with a significant year. "1969 - Moon Landing," read one tag. Another declared, "1980 - Who Shot J.R.?" Ruby grinned, realizing her uncle had found an unusual way to chronicle history—one pair of socks at a time. Each mismatched pair represented a moment in time, like a quirky timeline stitched together in fabric, as though he marked the passing of history not with dates on a calendar but with the most unexpected keepsakes.

The living room yielded a bookshelf full of self-help books with increasingly ridiculous titles. "*How to Win Friends and Influence Yetis*," Ruby read aloud, shaking her head. "*The Secret Life of Sasquatch: Unveiling the Mystery*." She snorted. "Well, at least now I know where you got all your crazy ideas from."

As she worked, Ruby found her irritation giving way to

amusement, and even a touch of fondness. Each item, no matter how useless, told a story about her uncle—his interests, his sense of humor, his unique way of looking at the world.

In the den, she stumbled upon what might have been Uncle Peter's pièce de résistance: a collection of snow globes, each containing a different gnome scene. Ruby picked one up, giving it a shake. Inside, tiny gnomes rode even tinier bicycles through a swirl of glittery snow.

"Gnomes on Bikes," read the label on the base. Next to it stood "Gnome Tea Party," "Gnomes Go Fishing," and—Ruby's personal favorite—"Gnome Sweet Gnome," featuring a gnome family gathered around a miniature television.

"Oh, Uncle Peter," Ruby said fondly, placing the snow globes on a shelf. "You were one of a kind, weren't you?"

Just then, a commotion outside caught her attention. Ruby moved to the window just in time to see Houdini making another bid for freedom, with Becket in hot pursuit.

"Oh no, not again," Ruby groaned, though her words carried more delight than annoyance. She watched as Becket caught up to the troublemaker, scooping him up with both exasperation and affection.

Ruby was tempted to go outside and help, but the task at hand was too important. With a sigh, she turned back to her search.

The kitchen yielded its own treasures—or rather, its own unique brand of useless items. The drawers were stuffed with takeout menus from restaurants that had long since closed. *"Pete's Palindrome Pizza - We deliver forwards and backwards!"* one proclaimed. Another advertised, *"The Upside-Down Cafe - Where the floor is the ceiling, and the prices are upside down too!"*

"Did you ever cook a meal in your life, Uncle Peter?" Ruby muttered, adding the menus to the growing pile of junk.

In a cupboard above the stove, she found a collection of novelty mugs. "I Believe in Bigfoot (He Believes in You Too)," read one. Another declared, "Aliens Abducted My Diet Plan." Ruby imagined her uncle sipping his morning coffee from these ridiculous cups.

As the day wore on, Ruby's search became increasingly desperate. She'd been through most of the house and had yet to find anything of real value. The pile of quirky, useless items had grown, but her hopes of finding something to sell had dwindled.

Just as she was about to give up, Ruby noticed a corner of something poking out from under a pile of old newspapers. Curious, she tugged at it, revealing a large, ornate trunk. It was locked, but the key hung from a piece of twine tied to the handle.

Ruby's heart raced as she turned the key. This was it—this had to be where Uncle Peter kept his valuables. She lifted the lid, already envisioning the treasures within.

What she found instead was a trunk full of old takeout menus and a scrapbook labeled "UFO Sightings (Probably)."

"You have got to be kidding me," Ruby groaned, flipping through the scrapbook. Page after page was filled with blurry photos of what were just lens flares and oddly shaped clouds. Uncle Peter's excited notes filled the margins: "Possible alien craft over Johnson's cow pasture?" and "Martian scout ship or unusually reflective weather balloon?"

At the back of the scrapbook, Ruby found an envelope. Her heart leapt, hoping it might contain forgotten cash or bonds. Instead, she pulled out a series of crayon drawings—

childish scribbles of UFOs and stick-figure aliens. With a jolt, Ruby recognized her own handiwork from when she was little.

"You kept these?" she asked, her fingers tracing the faded drawings. Her breath hitched as she realized how much these silly pictures must have meant to her uncle.

Ruby slumped against the trunk, feeling both defeat and unexpected emotion. She'd spent the entire day searching and had nothing to show for it except a newfound appreciation for her uncle's eccentricities—and a reminder of the connection they'd shared, however brief.

From outside, Becket's laughter rang out, followed by a chorus of bleats. Ruby shook her head, her frustration fading as she made her way to the window, watching as Becket led his little herd back to their pen.

As she observed him, Ruby was struck by how at home he looked here. In just a few short days, Becket and his goats had become as much a part of the landscape as the mountains in the distance. And if she was being honest with herself, she was starting to feel the same way.

The thought both thrilled and terrified her. This wasn't the plan. She was supposed to come here, sell the house, and get back to her real life in Chicago. But with each passing day, the idea of returning to her tiny apartment and endless freelance gigs seemed less and less appealing.

"What am I doing?" Ruby muttered, resting her forehead against the cool glass of the window. She thought about the townsfolk—how they'd welcomed her with open arms, how they'd laughed off Houdini's antics instead of getting angry. She thought about Becket, with his laid-back nature and that wild idea of goat landscaping.

And she thought about Uncle Peter. His presence lingered in every corner of the house—in the quirky collections, the bizarre books, the years of accumulated memories. For the first time, Ruby felt truly connected to the uncle she had never fully known.

With a deep breath, Ruby straightened up. She might not have found anything valuable to sell, but that didn't mean she was giving up. She'd made a promise to the town, and she was going to keep it—one way or another.

"Alright, Aspen Cove," she said, a determined glint in her eye. "Let's see what we can do about those decorations."

As the sun began to set, painting the snow-covered landscape in shades of pink and gold, Ruby settled at the kitchen table with a notepad and pen. It was time to get creative. She might not have money, but she had two hands, a whole house full of weird and wonderful junk, and a town full of people who seemed willing to give her a chance.

A knock at the door interrupted her brainstorming. She opened it to find Becket, his cheeks red from the cold, a hesitant look on his face.

"Hey," he said, stamping the snow from his boots. "Just wanted to check in. How'd the treasure hunt go?"

Ruby sighed, stepping back to let him in. "Well, if I ever need a souvenir spoon from a country I've never visited, I'm all set. Otherwise..." She shrugged, leading him into the kitchen.

Becket's eyes widened as he took in the piles of odds and ends scattered around the room. "Wow. Your uncle sure liked to collect things, huh?"

"That's one way of putting it," Ruby picked up one of the gnome snow globes, giving it a shake. "Want to see the pride of his collection?"

As she showed Becket the various gnome scenes, explaining each one with increasing amusement, the tension of the day began to ease for Ruby. Soon, they were both laughing, coming up with ridiculous backstories for each one.

"You know," Becket said, setting down "Gnomes Go Fishing," "these are kind of cute. In a weird way."

Ruby nodded, surprised to find herself agreeing. "Yeah, they are. I think I'm going to keep them. A little piece of Uncle Peter's particular brand of crazy."

They lapsed into a comfortable silence, the kitchen growing dim as the last of the daylight faded. Ruby was acutely aware of Becket's presence, of the way he seemed to fill the space, bringing a sense of comfort that had nothing to do with the heating.

"So," he said, nodding towards her notepad. "What's the plan?"

Ruby took a deep breath. "I'm not sure yet. But I'm going to figure it out. I made a promise to this town, and I intend to keep it."

Becket's eyes crinkled at the corners. "I don't doubt it for a second. And hey, if you need any help—or if you decide those gnomes would make good Christmas decorations—just let me know."

As he turned to leave, Ruby called out, "Becket?"

He paused at the door, looking back at her.

"Thanks," she said. "For everything."

His face brightened. "Anytime, Ruby. Anytime."

After he left, Ruby turned back to her notepad, feeling re-energized. Tomorrow, she decided, she'd start making calls. Maybe Katie from the bakery would have some ideas. Or Doc Parker—he seemed to know everyone and everything in town.

For the first time since Houdini's escapade, Ruby sensed that things might start to turn around. As she jotted down ideas, she realized that somewhere along the way, making things right with the town had become about more than just fulfilling a hasty promise. It had become about finding her place in Aspen Cove.

She paused, letting that thought sink in. She'd come here with every intention of leaving, but something was changing. As she glanced at the gnome snow globes, now arranged proudly on the kitchen windowsill, Ruby wondered if she was already halfway there. Was it possible for her to have a future here?

As night fell, Ruby stayed at the kitchen table, surrounded by the remnants of Uncle Peter's life. She picked up a UFO photo, smiling at the enthusiastic scribbles in the margins. It struck her how much life he had lived in this house—how many dreams he'd chased, how many adventures he'd imagined. And now, somehow, she was a part of it too.

And here she was, ready to sell it all off without a second thought.

The realization made her pause. Was she truly so eager to erase all traces of Uncle Peter from her life? To turn her back on this town that had welcomed her with open arms?

Ruby glanced out the window, where she could just make out the shape of Becket's tent in the moonlight. She thought about how fast he'd come to her aid, how he'd faced down the town's judgment without hesitation. How he'd made her laugh even in the midst of crisis.

With a sigh, Ruby closed her notebook. She had a lot to think about, and not just about Christmas decorations. As she got ready for bed, she found herself humming a tune— something she hadn't done in months.

CHAPTER TWELVE

The wind howled around Becket's tent, pulling him from sleep. He blinked in the dim light, momentarily disoriented. The air inside the tent was frigid, his breath visible in small puffs. The sleeping bag that had seemed so cozy when he'd fallen asleep now offered little protection against the biting cold.

"Well, this is new," he muttered, sitting up and rubbing his hands together. His fingers were stiff, and he flexed them, wincing at the pins and needles sensation.

Unzipping the tent flap, Becket was met with a wall of white. Snow was falling heavily, obscuring everything beyond a few feet. The wind whipped the flakes into a frenzy, creating swirling patterns in the air. It was beautiful, in a terrifying sort of way.

"Ah, hell," Becket groaned, zipping the tent back up. This was more than just a light dusting. This was a full-blown winter storm, the kind that could strand people for days if they weren't prepared. And he was most definitely not prepared.

Concern for his goats immediately overrode his own

discomfort. Becket hurriedly pulled on his boots and coat, fumbling with the tent's zipper before stepping out into the maelstrom. He braced himself, taking a deep breath of icy air as the wind threatened to knock him off his feet.

Trudging towards the makeshift pen, Becket could hear the distressed bleating rising above the howling wind, tugging at his heart. Snow had piled up against the sides, and he cursed himself for not checking the weather. "I'm coming, guys!" he called out, though his voice was lost to the storm.

The snow crunched beneath his boots, already several inches deep, when a brown and white head popped up over a snowdrift—Houdini, of course. The escape artist had climbed the snow pile and perched precariously atop the pen, looking for all the world like the king of a small, cold mountain.

"Don't you dare," Becket warned, quickening his pace. He could already see the playful glint in the goat's eye, the one that always preceded trouble.

But it was too late. With a triumphant bleat that sounded almost like a laugh, Houdini leapt from his snowy perch ... and immediately sank up to his neck in the deep snow beyond the pen. The look of surprise on the goat's face was almost comical.

Despite the seriousness of the situation, Becket laughed at the goat's startled expression. "Not quite the great escape you had in mind, huh buddy?" Even in a crisis, Houdini managed to lighten the mood.

Scooping up Houdini, Becket made his way to the pen's entrance. The goat's wet fur soaked through his gloves, making his already cold hands even colder. Inside the pen, the rest of the herd was huddled together, looking cold and weary. Daisy, heavy with her pregnancy, looked downright uncomfortable.

"Alright, gang," Becket said, assessing the situation. His mind raced, trying to come up with a solution. "This isn't going to work. We need to find you someplace warmer." He ran a hand through his hair, dislodging a small shower of snowflakes.

He glanced toward Ruby's house. The porch light was on, casting a warm glow through the swirling snow. Becket was tempted to knock on her door, to ask for shelter. The thought of being inside, warm and dry, was incredibly appealing. But he dismissed the idea. He couldn't impose on her like that, not after all the trouble Houdini had caused. Besides, he was used to handling things.

"Looks like we're on our own, guys," he told the goats, trying to sound more confident than he was. "Let's see what we can rig up."

Over the next hour, Becket battled the elements as he attempted to construct a more substantial shelter for his herd. He used tarps from his truck, spare pieces of wood he found scattered around the yard, and no small amount of creativity. The wind bit at his exposed skin, and his hands grew numb despite his gloves. But he pressed on, driven by the need to protect his animals.

But the wind kept tearing down his efforts, and the snow was accumulating faster than he could clear it. Every time he thought he was making progress, a gust would come along and undo all his hard work. It was like trying to build a house of cards in a wind tunnel.

Exhausted and half-frozen, Becket had to admit defeat. His clothes were soaked through, his teeth chattering uncontrollably. He couldn't leave the goats out here, not in this weather. They needed real shelter, and fast. As much as he hated to admit it, he needed help.

With a heavy heart, Becket made his way to Ruby's door. He hesitated before knocking, acutely aware of his snow-covered appearance and the early hour. What if she turned him away? What if she was angry at being woken up? He pushed the thoughts aside. He had to try, for the goats' sake.

After what seemed like an eternity, the door opened. Ruby stood there in flannel pajamas and an oversized sweater, her hair a mess and her eyes still heavy with sleep. But as soon as she saw Becket, those eyes widened with concern.

"Becket? What's wrong? Are you okay?"

Becket opened his mouth to explain, but a strong gust of wind chose that moment to blow him off balance. Ruby reached out, grabbing his arm to steady him. Her touch, even through his wet coat, was warm.

"Get in here," she said, pulling him inside and shutting the door against the storm. "You're freezing!"

As Becket stepped inside, the heat of the house hit him, and his frozen fingers began to tingle painfully. "Thanks," he managed through chattering teeth. "It's the goats. They can't stay out there in this storm. I tried to build them a shelter, but..."

Understanding dawned on Ruby's face. "Say no more. We'll figure something out."

Relief washed over Becket. He should have known Ruby would understand. In the short time he'd known her, she'd proven herself to be kind and resourceful. "I hate to impose," he started, but Ruby cut him off with a wave of her hand.

"Don't be ridiculous. We can't leave them out there. Now, let's think. Where can we put a bunch of goats?"

Becket's eyes swept over the clutter—piles of books, odd knick-knacks, and the inexplicable garden gnomes. Definitely not goat territory, but his mind kept turning.

"Well," Becket said with a half-smile, "any chance your uncle left you a barn tucked away somewhere?"

Ruby sighed dramatically. "Nope. Guess we'll just have to bring them all inside."

Becket raised an eyebrow. "You're kidding, right?"

Ruby grinned. "It's not the worst idea. But..." Her face lit up as inspiration struck. "The garage! It's full of junk, but it's got a roof and walls. We could clear enough space for the goats."

Becket nodded, already moving towards the door. The prospect of action, of having a plan, energized him. "It's worth a shot. Let's do it."

The next few hours were a blur of activity. Becket and Ruby braved the storm multiple times, ferrying goats from the pen to the garage. The wind howled around them, snow pelting their faces, but they pressed on. Inside, they cleared space, stacking boxes and shoving old furniture aside to create a makeshift goat hotel. To keep the biting cold at bay, they led each goat in through the side door that opened to the yard, leaving the big garage door firmly shut. The third door, leading into the kitchen, offered a welcome escape to warmth between trips.

By the time they got the last goat settled, both Becket and Ruby were exhausted, covered in snow, and laughing at the absurdity of it all. Becket couldn't remember the last time he'd laughed this much, especially in the face of adversity.

"I can't believe we just turned your garage into a goat

barn," Becket said, watching as Houdini immediately started investigating his new surroundings, nosing at boxes and trying to chew on an old tennis racket.

Ruby grinned, reaching out to scratch behind Daisy's ears. The pregnant goat leaned into her touch, looking far more content than she had in the pen. "Wait until the HOA hears about this. Oh wait, we don't have one of those out here, do we?"

Their laughter was interrupted by a loud rumble. Becket looked down at his stomach, embarrassed. "Sorry. Guess all this goat wrangling worked up an appetite."

"Come on," Ruby said, heading towards the house. "I think we've earned some breakfast. I make a mean scrambled egg."

As they stepped back into the house, Becket marveled at how natural it felt—working side by side, tackling problems, laughing in the face of adversity. It was as if they'd known each other for years, not days. He watched Ruby walk ahead, admiring her determination, her spirit, and the way each step radiated confidence and purpose.

In the kitchen, Ruby busied herself with making breakfast while Becket sat at the table, warming his hands around a mug of coffee. The storm continued to rage outside, but in here, everything was calm and cozy. The contrast was striking, and for the first time in months, Becket experienced a sense of peace settling over him.

"You know," Ruby said as she set a plate of steaming eggs in front of him, "I think Uncle Peter would have loved this. Turning his garage into a goat sanctuary? That's right up his alley of weirdness."

Becket dug into the eggs with gusto. They were delicious, perfectly seasoned and fluffy. "From what you've told me about him, I think you're right. He sounds like he was quite a character."

"That he was," Ruby agreed. "I wish I'd known him better."

They ate in comfortable silence for a while, the only sounds being the clink of forks against plates and the howling of the wind outside. Becket glanced at Ruby, admiring the way the morning light played across her features.

"Listen, Ruby," Becket said, setting down his fork. "I can't thank you enough for this. For helping with the goats, for breakfast, for everything." A lump formed in his throat, overwhelmed by her kindness.

Ruby met his eyes, her expression soft. "That's what friends do, right? Help each other out?"

Friends. The word warmed Becket more than the coffee ever could. "Right," he agreed. "Friends." But even as he said it, he wondered if that word fully encompassed what he was beginning to feel for Ruby.

As the day wore on and the storm showed no signs of letting up, they settled into an easy routine. They checked on the goats regularly, played board games unearthed from Uncle Peter's collection, and talked for hours about everything and nothing.

Becket spoke more openly than he had in years, sharing stories about his life on the farm, his dreams for the future. Ruby listened attentively, asking thoughtful questions and sharing her own experiences. With each passing hour, the connection between them grew stronger.

By the time evening rolled around, he realized he hadn't once thought about leaving. The idea of going back to his cold, lonely tent seemed almost absurd now. And when Ruby suggested he take the guest room for the night instead of braving the storm to return to his tent, he found himself agreeing without hesitation.

Becket relaxed as he lay in bed that night, listening to the wind outside and the occasional distant bleat from the garage. This wasn't how he'd planned to weather the storm, but somehow, it seemed right.

His last thought before drifting off to sleep was that he'd found more than just shelter from the storm in Aspen Cove. Maybe he'd found a place he could call home. And perhaps, he'd found someone he wanted to share his life with.

CHAPTER THIRTEEN

The crack of splintering wood echoed through the house, followed by an all-too-familiar bleat. Ruby's head snapped up from the book she'd been reading, her eyes meeting Becket's across the living room. They stared at each other in stunned silence.

"Please tell me that wasn't what I think it was," Ruby groaned, already knowing the answer.

Becket was on his feet in an instant, moving towards the kitchen with Ruby close behind. They rounded the corner to find Daisy, the pregnant goat, standing triumphantly atop the kitchen table, surrounded by the remains of what had once been one of Uncle Peter's chairs.

"How did she even get in here?" Ruby exclaimed, torn between exasperation and admiration for the goat's determination.

Becket glanced at the door, still ajar. "We must not have shut the door all the way when we checked on them this morning. She probably nudged it open ... maybe she was looking for a snack."

Ruby's eyes widened. "You think she was after food?"

Becket shrugged. "She's eating for two... or more."

As they wrangled Daisy, trying to guide her off the table, a laugh bubbled out of Ruby. It was so ridiculous—here she was, in the middle of a blizzard, chasing a goat through her late uncle's kitchen. If someone had told her a week ago that this would be her life, she would have called them crazy.

"You know," Becket said as they finally managed to guide Daisy back towards the garage, "I think she's getting restless. The storm, the confinement ... it can't be easy for her, especially this far along in her pregnancy."

Ruby nodded, reaching out to scratch behind Daisy's ears. "Poor girl. I guess we're all feeling a bit cooped up, huh?"

As they walked back into the house, Ruby couldn't ignore Becket's presence—the way he moved, his laughter, the occasional brush of his arm against hers. It was distracting, to say the least.

Back in the kitchen, they surveyed the scene of Daisy's latest escapade. The broken chair lay in pieces on the floor, proof of the surprising strength of a determined goat.

"Well," Ruby sighed, "I guess we know what we're doing this afternoon."

They set about cleaning up the mess, working together in comfortable silence. As they worked, Ruby found her mind wandering. She thought about how Becket had become a part of her daily life, how natural it felt to have him around. It was unsettling, in a way. She'd come to Aspen Cove with a clear plan: sell the house, tie up loose ends, and get back to her real life in Chicago. Becket and his goats weren't part of that plan.

And yet...

"You okay there?" Becket's voice broke through her reverie. "You looked like you were a million miles away."

Ruby blinked, realizing she'd been staring blankly at a chair leg for who knows how long. "Oh, yeah, sorry. Just thinking."

Becket tilted his head, a curious expression on his face. "Penny for your thoughts?"

Ruby was tempted to tell him everything. About her plans to sell, about her conflicted feelings, about how he was making her question everything she thought she wanted. "Just wondering how I'm going to explain to the next owners why there are hoof prints on the kitchen table."

Becket laughed, but Ruby thought she glimpsed something—disappointment? Before she could dwell on it, a gust of wind rattled the windows, reminding them of the storm still raging outside.

"We should check the weather report," Becket suggested. "See how long this storm's going to last."

The news wasn't good. The blizzard showed no signs of letting up, with forecasts predicting at least another day of heavy snow and high winds.

"Looks like you might be stuck with us for a while longer," Becket said, a hint of uncertainty in his voice. "If that's okay, I mean. We could try to find somewhere else—"

"Don't be ridiculous," Ruby cut him off, surprising herself with the vehemence in her tone. "Of course you're staying here. Where else would you go in this weather?"

Relief washed over Becket's face. "Thanks, Ruby."

As the day wore on, they settled into their usual rhythm. They made regular trips to check on the goats, played a heated game of Scrabble where Becket insisted that "zoink" was a word and Ruby vehemently disagreed, and kept an eye on the ever-worsening storm.

In the afternoon, they decided to tackle some of the clutter in the living room, hoping to clear more space. As they sorted through box after box of Uncle Peter's eclectic collection, Ruby shared stories she hadn't thought about in years.

"And this," she said, holding up a snow globe with a miniature Bigfoot inside, "was from the summer Uncle Peter swore he saw Bigfoot while camping. He came back with a plaster cast of a footprint and everything."

Becket laughed, his eyes twinkling. "And? Was it real?"

Ruby grinned. "Turned out to be a bear print. But Uncle Peter never admitted it. He kept insisting that Bigfoot just happened to have bear-like feet."

As they worked, Ruby opened up more and more. She told Becket about her childhood visits to Aspen Cove, her dreams of becoming an artist, and the soul-crushing reality of her corporate job in Chicago. Becket listened attentively, asking questions and sharing his own experiences.

"So, what made you decide to quit?" he asked as they took a break, sitting on the floor surrounded by half-empty boxes and piles of knick-knacks.

Ruby sighed, fiddling with a paperweight shaped like a UFO. "I just ... couldn't do it anymore, you know? Spending my days in a cubicle, working on projects I didn't care about."

Becket nodded, understanding in his eyes. "That's brave, though. Taking that leap."

Ruby snorted. "Brave or stupid. The jury's still out on that one."

"Hey," Becket said, reaching out to touch her hand. "For what it's worth, I think it was brave. And I think you're doing great."

The sincerity in his voice made Ruby's heart skip a beat. She looked up, meeting his gaze, and the world seemed to narrow to just the two of them.

The moment was broken by a sudden power dip, the lights dimming before coming back to full brightness. Ruby and Becket looked at each other, a hint of worry in their eyes.

"That can't be good," Ruby muttered, getting to her feet. "Let's prepare for a potential outage."

They spent the next hour gathering candles, flashlights, and extra blankets, all the while keeping an anxious eye on the lights. Just as they finished their preparations, the power went out, plunging the house into darkness.

"Well," Becket's voice came from somewhere to Ruby's left, "I guess we were right to be prepared."

As Ruby fumbled for a flashlight, her hand brushed against Becket's in the darkness. The touch sent a jolt through her, and she was acutely aware of how close they were standing.

"Ruby?" Becket's voice was soft, uncertain.

Before she could respond, a loud crash came from the direction of the garage, followed by a chorus of alarmed bleats.

"The goats!" they said in unison, all thoughts of the moment forgotten as they rushed to check on their four-legged guests.

As they navigated the darkened house with flashlights in hand, Ruby couldn't help but reflect on the situation. This wasn't how she'd envisioned her time in Aspen Cove, but somehow, amid the chaos and uncertainty, she found herself feeling more alive than she had in years.

And as for Becket? Well, that was something she'd have

to figure out. But for now, as they faced the darkness and whatever goat-related crisis awaited them together, Ruby knew one thing for certain: she was where she wanted to be.

CHAPTER FOURTEEN

The muffled sound of an engine struggling against the snow drifted into the room, pulling Becket from sleep. He blinked, momentarily disoriented by the unfamiliar surroundings of Ruby's spare room. Then the events of the past few days came rushing back—the storm, moving the goats into the garage, the lights turning off, the long, cold night, and then the relief when power was finally restored.

Ruby's unwavering support through it all had been a bright spot in the chaos. The heat of the house now felt like a luxury after those tense hours in the cold.

He stumbled to the window, rubbing sleep from his eyes, and squinted at the old pickup truck making its way up the snow-covered driveway. The vehicle was unfamiliar, but that didn't mean much. He didn't know anyone in town but Ruby and the few people he'd come across. Curiosity piqued, Becket dressed and made his way to the kitchen.

As he entered, he almost collided with Ruby, who was emerging with two steaming mugs of coffee.

"Whoa there, Goat Whisperer," she laughed, deftly

maneuvering to avoid spilling. "I was just coming to wake you. Looks like we have a visitor."

Becket accepted the offered mug gratefully, inhaling the rich aroma. "Any idea who it is?"

Ruby shook her head, peering out the window. "No clue. I'm still getting used to the idea that people just show up unannounced out here. In Chicago, unexpected visitors usually meant you forgot to pay a bill."

Becket laughed. "Small town life is a bit different. Could be someone in trouble, or someone coming to help. Or just a neighbor being nosy."

"Well, as long as it's not bill collectors," Ruby said. "I'm not sure I'm ready for that level of small-town hospitality just yet."

A knock at the door cut through their banter. Exchanging glances, they moved to the entrance. Ruby opened it to reveal a tall, weathered man with kind eyes and a snow-dusted hat.

"Mornin', Ruby," the man said. "Hope I'm not disturbing you too early. My name's Cade Mosier." He tipped his hat to Becket. "You must be our new goat wrangler. Heard you might be needin' some help with the storm and all."

"Pleased to meet you, Mr. Mosier," Becket said, shaking the man's hand. "What brings you out in this weather?"

Cade's eyes crinkled. "Well, Doc Parker mentioned you folks were new in town and might be needin' some help. It got me wondering about those goats of yours. Do they have a proper shelter?"

Becket and Ruby exchanged glances. "We've moved them into the garage for now," Becket explained. "Not ideal, but it's better than leaving them outside in this weather."

"Smart thinking." Cade nodded approvingly. "Thought

you might be runnin' low on feed, what with your goats cooped up and all. Brought some hay and feed, if you're interested."

A wave of gratitude washed over Becket. He'd been worried sick about how he was going to feed his goats if the snow didn't melt soon. "That's incredibly kind of you. I can't tell you how much I appreciate it. How much do I owe you?"

Cade waved him off. "Don't you worry about that. This is Aspen Cove, and we take care of our own."

"But we're not—" Becket started to protest but was cut off by Ruby's elbow nudging his ribs.

"What my friend here means to say," Ruby said, "is that we're incredibly grateful. Why don't you come in for a cup of coffee, Cade? It's freezing out there."

As they walked to the kitchen, Becket grinned. "You know, Ruby suggested we should bring the goats inside. I'm not sure she quite gets how spectacularly bad of an idea that would be."

Ruby rolled her eyes, but her lips twitched with amusement. "Hey, I just figured they could eat half the junk I've been sorting through. It'd cut my workload down." Then she paused, a look of mock horror crossing her face. "Although ... I didn't think about what goes in must come out. Maybe not my brightest idea."

Cade let out a hearty laugh. "I'd pay good money to see a house full of goats. Might make for some interesting decorating, that's for sure."

Ruby shook her head. "I can imagine. Though I suppose it can't be any stranger than what I found going through the boxes here."

"Oh, you ain't seen nothing yet," Cade said. "Wait till you meet Mrs. Brown and her cat, Piddles."

Becket and Ruby exchanged curious glances. "Mrs. Brown?" Becket asked.

Cade nodded, enjoying the chance to introduce the newcomers to some local color. "Lives just down the road. Sweet lady, but she's got some unique ideas. And let's just say, her cat Piddles is the best-dressed feline in the county."

"Best-dressed cat?" Ruby repeated, her eyebrows rising.

"Oh yeah," Cade said. "Mrs. Brown dresses that cat up in outfits. Wait till you see Piddles in his Christmas sweater. It's quite the sight."

As they settled around the kitchen table with steaming mugs of coffee, Cade regaled them with tales of Aspen Cove's colorful residents. Becket was surprised by how quickly the atmosphere warmed, their conversation flowing easily despite their recent acquaintance. He and Ruby listened with a mix of amusement and amazement, getting their first real taste of the quirky community they'd stumbled into. Despite its strangeness, it seemed right.

Over coffee, Cade filled them in on the town gossip. Becket alternated between amazement at the townspeople's generosity and amusement at their quirks. There was Doc Parker, who made his rounds in his ancient truck, affectionately called "The Blue Goose," which, according to Cade, "sounded like a herd of dyspeptic elk."

"The Blue Goose made it through all this snow?" Becket asked, impressed.

Cade nodded, a twinkle in his eye. "Oh, that old truck's seen worse. Doc swears it's got more lives than Mrs. Brown's cat. Speaking of which, do you want to hear about Piddles' latest adventure?"

Ruby listened with growing fascination as Cade regaled them with the tale of how Piddles, decked out in his new sailor outfit, had somehow gotten stuck on Mrs. Brown's roof during the storm. It had taken the combined efforts of Doc Parker, his trusty Blue Goose, the fire department and half the town to rescue the fashion-forward feline.

"I can't believe how everyone helps each other," Ruby said, shaking her head in wonder. "In Chicago, I didn't know my neighbors' names, let alone their pets' wardrobe malfunctions."

"That's just how we do things around here," Cade said with a nod. "Oh, and speaking of local color, did you know we've got ourselves a bit of a celebrity in town?"

Ruby leaned forward, intrigued. "A celebrity? Here in Aspen Cove?"

"Sure do," Cade nodded. "Samantha, though you might know her better as Indigo. Lives out by the lake."

Ruby's jaw dropped. "Indigo? The pop star? She lives here?"

Becket watched Ruby's excitement with a grin. He'd heard of the singer, sure, but hadn't realized just how much Ruby was a fan.

"Oh yeah," Cade confirmed. "She's good people. Even performed at last year's Christmas festival. Caused quite a stir, let me tell you." They walked toward the door. "Oh, speaking of Christmas," Cade added, "the annual cookie exchange is coming up soon. You two should join us."

"Cookie exchange?" Ruby asked.

Cade nodded enthusiastically. "It's quite the event. Everyone gathers on Main Street with their homemade cookies. Maisey supplies hot cocoa, and Katie from the bakery brings warm brownies. We do the Christmas lighting ceremony that day too. It's a big deal around here."

"Sounds wonderful," Ruby said, her eyes lighting up. "What do you think, Becket?"

Becket hesitated, then surprised himself by saying,

"That sounds like fun. Though I have to warn you, my baking skills are a bit rusty."

Ruby's eyebrows shot up. "Baking skills? Is there anything you can't do, Becket?"

He grinned. "Well, I'm terrible at knitting. So, if we get stranded again, we'll have to rely on Mrs. Brown for our sweater needs."

The cold air was bracing after the heat of the kitchen, and Becket welcomed it, hoping it would clear his head.

"You know," Cade said as they hefted a bale of hay, "it's good to see lights on in this old place again. Are you staying for a while, then?"

Becket hesitated. He knew Ruby's original plan had been to sell the house and leave, but after the past few days … "I'm not sure," he admitted. "I hope so."

Cade's eyes twinkled knowingly. "Well, between you and me, you seem good for each other." He clapped Becket on the shoulder. "Don't let a good thing slip away, you hear?"

After Cade left, he thought about the cowboy's easy generosity, about Doc Parker braving the storm in his Blue Goose to check on people, about Mrs. Brown and her fashionable feline. He thought about Ruby, throwing herself into goat care with enthusiasm and determination.

He thought about her laugh, the way her eyes lit up at the mention of Indigo, the determination with which she tackled every challenge. Without realizing it, Ruby had carved out a space for herself in his life, and Becket was starting to hope it might be permanent.

"What do you think, Houdini?" he asked, scratching the troublemaker's ears. "Should I tell her how I feel?"

Houdini bleated, butting his head against Becket's hand.

"Yeah, you're right," Becket said. "It's probably too soon. But maybe…"

His thoughts were interrupted by the creaking of the garage door as it opened. Ruby poked her head in, her cheeks flushed from the cold.

"Hey, Goat Whisperer," she called. "Need any help in here?"

Becket grinned, ignoring the way his heart skipped a beat at her appearance. "Always. Though I'm not sure Houdini approves of my distribution methods. He keeps giving me the stink eye because I gave Daisy more, but she's eating for two."

Ruby laughed, making her way through the goat-filled garage. "Well, you know what they say. You can't please all of the goats all of the time."

As they worked together, feeding and checking on each goat, Becket appreciated how natural it all was. Here he was, in a new town, in the garage of a house that wasn't even his, surrounded by near-strangers who had embraced him without hesitation. And at the center of it all was Ruby, transforming from reluctant house owner to enthusiastic goat co-parent in just a matter of days.

"Ruby," he said, surprising himself. "I … I wanted to thank you. For everything you've done. For the goats, for me … for making me feel welcome here."

Ruby paused in her task of refilling water buckets, her expression softening. "You don't have to thank me, Becket. I'm just glad I could help. And honestly?" She grinned. "I'm having more fun than I've had in years. Who knew goat farming could be so exciting?"

There was a moment of silence, full of unspoken words and rising tension. Becket stepped toward her, feeling an invisible pull.

"Ruby, I—"

But before he could finish, Daisy let out a loud bleat, startling them both. Ruby burst into laughter, her voice filling the garage and warming Becket's heart.

"I think someone's jealous of all the attention Houdini's getting," she said, moving to pet Daisy.

Becket watched her. He wasn't ready to put his feelings into words just yet, but he knew one thing for certain: whatever happened next, he wanted Ruby to be a part of it.

As they finished up in the garage and made their way back to the house, a sense of possibility stirred within Becket—something he hadn't experienced in years.

CHAPTER FIFTEEN

Ruby closed the garage door behind them, the coziness of the house a welcome relief after tending to the goats. The morning's excitement with Cade's visit and the delivery had left her stomach growling. She was struck by how naturally she'd adapted to this new routine, a stark contrast to her life in Chicago just a week ago.

"I don't know about you," she said, turning to Becket, "but I'm starving. We never got around to breakfast. How about I make us something?"

Becket's eyes lit up, and a spark ignited in Ruby at his boyish grin. "Breakfast sounds amazing. What can I do to help?"

Ruby was about to answer when a loud crash from the garage made them both jump. They exchanged alarmed glances before rushing back to the door. The concern in Becket's eyes mirrored her own, and a surge of protectiveness rose in Ruby for the goats she had come to care for in such a short time.

"Houdini," they said in unison, already knowing the culprit.

The scene that greeted them was one of utter chaos. Somehow, Houdini had managed to knock over a stack of boxes, scattering their contents across the floor. The other goats were taking full advantage of the situation, nibbling on papers and investigating the newly exposed treasures.

"Oh no," Ruby groaned, taking in the mess. "Uncle Peter's stuff. I hadn't sorted through these boxes yet." A pang of guilt hit her as she realized how much of her uncle's life she'd been planning to simply pack away and sell.

Becket was already moving, shooing goats away from the debris. "Come on, let's get this cleaned up before they eat something they shouldn't."

As they worked to contain the chaos, laughter escaped Ruby at the absurdity of it all. Here she was, in her deceased uncle's garage, rescuing his belongings from a group of goats. The laughter bubbled up from somewhere deep inside her, a release of tension she hadn't realized she'd been holding.

"What's so funny?" Becket asked as he wrestled a soggy newspaper away from one of the smaller goats.

"All of this." Ruby gestured around them, her eyes dancing with mirth. "A week ago, I was sitting in my apartment in Chicago, wondering how I was going to pay my rent. Now I'm here, playing goat rodeo with a bunch of escaped farm animals and a sexy stranger."

The words were out of her mouth before she could stop them. Ruby's cheeks heated as Becket stared at her. She'd been trying so hard to keep her growing attraction to him under wraps, and now she'd gone and blurted it out like a teenager with a crush.

"Sexy stranger, huh?" he said, a teasing look in his eye that made Ruby's heart skip a beat.

Ruby opened her mouth to backpedal, but was saved by

Daisy, who chose that moment to let out a loud bleat. Grateful for the distraction, Ruby turned her attention to the pregnant goat.

"Hey there, Daisy," she said, approaching the animal. "How are you feeling, mama?"

As she stroked Daisy's side, feeling the slight movements of the kid inside, Ruby was struck by a wave of emotion. She'd never considered herself an animal person, but there was something about these goats, about Daisy in particular, that touched her heart. The idea of leaving them when she sold the house seemed unbearable.

"She likes you," Becket said, coming to stand beside her. His proximity sent a shiver down Ruby's spine that had nothing to do with the cold.

"Yeah, well, the feeling's mutual," Ruby admitted, surprised by the thickness in her voice. "I never thought I'd say this, but I'm going to miss these guys when..." She trailed off, uncertain.

When what? When she sold the house and left? The thought, which had seemed so certain just days ago, now filled her with an unexpected sadness. Ruby pushed the feeling aside, focusing instead on the task at hand.

As they continued to sort through the scattered items, a glossy magazine caught Ruby's eye. She picked it up, her eyes widening as she realized what she was holding.

"Um, Becket?" she called out, her voice full of disbelief. "I think I just found Uncle Peter's dirty little secret."

Becket made his way over, his eyebrows rising as he saw the *Playboy* magazine in Ruby's hands. "Well," he said, clearing his throat, "I guess your uncle was a man of ... varied interests."

Ruby snorted, already digging through the box for more. "Varied is one word for it. Holy cow, there must be dozens of these. And look at the dates! Some of them go way back."

As they continued to sort through the magazines, Ruby's mind began to race. She'd heard stories about vintage magazines being worth money. Could these be valuable? Hope ignited in her chest.

"Becket," she said, an idea forming, "do you think these could be worth something? I mean, they're in good condition, and some of them are old..."

Becket nodded thoughtfully. "It's possible. Collectors pay good money for vintage magazines, especially if they're rare issues. We'd need to do some research to be sure, but..." He trailed off. "Ruby, this could be the solution to your decoration problem."

Excitement coursed through Ruby's veins. This could be it—the answer to her promise to replace the town's Christmas decorations. She looked up at Becket, finding his eyes already on her, filled with something that made her breath catch in her throat.

They just stared at each other, the air between them charged with unspoken words and growing tension. Ruby leaned in, drawn by some invisible force.

A loud sneeze from Houdini broke the spell. Ruby blinked, suddenly aware of how close she and Becket had gotten. She cleared her throat, taking a step back, her heart pounding.

"Right," she said, her voice breathless. "We should, um, finish cleaning up. And then maybe we can start researching these magazines?"

Becket nodded, a slight flush on his cheeks. "Yeah, good idea. I'll take care of the goats if you want to gather up the goods."

Once the garage was under control, Ruby quickly

scrambled some eggs and made toast. They ate in a hurry, their conversation circling back to the newly unearthed *Playboy* collection. Between bites, Ruby found herself sneaking glances at Becket, surprised at how easily she felt at home around him, despite barely knowing him.

After breakfast, they gathered Uncle Peter's *Playboy* collection and brought it into the living room. As Ruby spread the magazines out on the coffee table, she realized that she wasn't just solving a problem for the town. She was, perhaps, finding a place for herself in this wonderful community. The thought both excited and terrified her.

The rest of the day passed in a flurry of activity. Ruby and Becket set up a makeshift research station, poring over collector websites on Ruby's laptop while sorting through the magazines. She enjoyed the easy camaraderie between them, the way they worked together seamlessly as if they'd known each other for years.

As evening fell, they sat surrounded by stacks of organized *Playboys*, a notepad filled with potential values and buyer contacts. Ruby leaned back on the couch, stretching her arms above her head, feeling a sense of accomplishment she hadn't experienced in a long time.

"I can't believe it," she said, a note of wonder in her voice. "If these estimates are right, we could have enough to replace all the decorations and then some."

Becket nodded, looking equally amazed. "Your uncle's, uh, hobby might just save Christmas for Aspen Cove."

Ruby laughed, the sound full and genuine. "Who would have thought? I come here to sell a house and end up saving Christmas with vintage porn."

Their laughter mingled in the warm air of the living room, and as Ruby looked at Becket, his eyes crinkled with mirth, a wave of affection washed over her. Without thinking, she reached out and placed her hand over his, marveling at how natural it felt.

"Thank you," she said, her voice thick with emotion. "For everything. I don't know what I would have done without you these past few days."

Becket's hand reached for hers, intertwining their fingers. The contact sent a shiver up Ruby's arm. "You've given me and my goats a home when we needed it most."

The air between them grew thick with unspoken words and restrained desire. Ruby's gaze dropped to Becket's lips, her breath catching as he moved closer. The space between them shrank with agonizing slowness, Ruby's heart pounding harder with every passing second.

Just as their lips were about to meet, a loud sound from the garage shattered the moment. They jumped apart, both laughing nervously, the tension broken but not forgotten.

"I better go check on them," Becket said, running a hand through his hair. Ruby found the gesture endearing.

Ruby nodded, trying to ignore the disappointment settling in her chest. "Yeah, of course. I'll ... I'll start on dinner?"

As Becket headed out to the garage, Ruby leaned back on the couch, her heart racing. She touched her fingers to her lips, imagining what it would feel like to kiss Becket.

With a sigh, she got up and headed to the kitchen, her mind swirling with thoughts of goats, *Playboys*, and a certain handsome goat farmer who was becoming much more than just a sexy stranger.

Becket grunted as he heaved another shovelful of snow from the driveway. The morning air was crisp and biting, his breath forming small clouds with each exhale. He'd been at it for over an hour, first cleaning up after the goats in the garage, then tackling the snow-covered walkways.

As he worked, his mind wandered to Ruby. He'd heard her moving around the house early this morning, the soft padding of her footsteps and the gentle click of her laptop keys. Whatever she was up to, it had her excited enough to forgo sleep.

Becket realized how attuned he'd become to Ruby's presence in such a short time. The way she hummed absently while lost in thought, the scent of her shampoo lingering in the hallway, her laughter echoing through the house—all of it had become as familiar and necessary to him as breathing.

He was so lost in his thoughts that he almost missed the creak of the front door opening.

"Becket!" Ruby called out, her voice brimming with excitement. "Come quick! I've got something to show you!"

Propping his shovel against the porch railing, Becket jogged towards the house, his heart racing—though whether from the exertion or the thrill in Ruby's voice, he couldn't be sure. Stamping the snow from his boots, he stepped inside, instantly greeted by the comforting scent of coffee and something distinctly Ruby.

He found her in the living room, laptop open and a triumphant grin on her face. Her hair was mussed, and Becket had to resist the urge to run his fingers through it. Instead, he focused on the excitement radiating from her eyes.

"What's got you so worked up this early?" he asked.

Ruby's grin widened. "I've been up all night working on this," she said, turning the laptop towards him. "Take a look."

Becket leaned in, his eyes widening as he took in the eBay listing on the screen. "You did all this overnight?"

Ruby nodded, practically bouncing with excitement. "I photographed and cataloged every single issue. My uncle had some seriously rare editions. There's one from 1953 that's apparently worth a small fortune on its own! It features Marilyn Monroe."

Becket shook his head in amazement. "Ruby, this is incredible. You must be exhausted."

She waved off his concern. "I'm running on pure adrenaline right now. Besides, this could be our chance to help the town. It's worth losing a little sleep over."

As they scrolled through the listing together, Becket was drawn in by Ruby's enthusiasm. Her dedication to helping Aspen Cove, a place she'd only just come to know, was just one of the many things he admired about her. He found himself stealing glances as she spoke, captivated by the way her eyes lit up and her hands moved animatedly. "So, what now?" he asked, leaning against the desk.

"Now, we wait," she said. "And hope that collectors are early risers."

The next few hours were a lesson in patience. They tried to distract themselves, Becket insisting that Ruby eat something and Ruby forcing Becket to take a break from his chores, but they both found their eyes drawn back to the laptop screen every few minutes.

"This is ridiculous," Ruby laughed after catching herself refreshing the page for the hundredth time. "We're acting like we're waiting for lottery results."

Becket moved to stand behind her chair. "Well, in a way, we are. This could change everything for you."

Just as the words left his mouth, a notification pinged on the laptop. They both froze, eyes locked on the screen.

"Is that...?" Becket started.

Ruby nodded, her hand shaking as she moved the mouse. "It's an offer. A big one."

The next hour passed in a blur of emails and phone calls. The buyer, a collector from New York, was eager to secure the entire collection. By the time they hung up the phone, the deal was done. The payment had been transferred, and all that was left was to package and ship the magazines.

"I can't believe it," Ruby said, her voice filled with wonder. "We did it, Becket. We did it!"

Without thinking, Becket pulled her into a hug. Ruby stiffened, then melted into his embrace. As they stood there, her body pressed against his, Becket knew he couldn't fight his feelings any longer.

He pulled back, his hands coming to rest on Ruby's

shoulders. Their eyes met, and the world seemed to stop spinning.

"Ruby," he said, his voice rough with emotion. "I..."

But words failed him. Instead, he leaned in, giving her time to pull away if she wanted. But Ruby met him halfway, her lips pressing against his in a kiss that set every nerve ending on fire.

It was soft at first, tentative, but deepened as days of pent-up longing and attraction poured out. Becket's hand cupped Ruby's cheek, while hers tangled in his hair. He pulled her closer, eliminating any space between them, reveling in the feel of her body against his.

Ruby's lips parted on a sigh, and Becket took the invitation, deepening the kiss. She tasted of coffee and something sweet, and Becket knew in that moment that he would never get enough of her. His hand slid down to the small of her back, pressing her even closer as Ruby's fingers tightened in his hair.

The kiss seemed to last forever and end too soon all at once. When they broke apart, both breathless, Becket rested his forehead against Ruby's.

"I've been wanting to do that for a while now," he admitted, his voice husky.

Ruby laughed, her eyes shining. "Me too. I was beginning to think you'd never make a move."

Becket grinned, feeling lighter than he had in years. "Well, I aim to make up for lost time."

He leaned in for another kiss, but a noise from the garage cut him off. They both burst into laughter.

"I swear, those goats have the worst timing," Ruby said, shaking her head.

Becket stepped back, though reluctantly. "I'll go see

what they're up to. But we're not done here," he added with a wink that made Ruby's cheeks flush.

As he tended to the goats, Becket's mind was already racing with plans. With the money from the *Playboy* sale, they could replace the town's decorations and make them even better. He found himself imagining future Christmases in Aspen Cove, with Ruby by his side. The thought filled him with a warmth that had nothing to do with the afternoon sun.

When he returned to the house, he found Ruby on the phone, discussing rush shipping for new decorations.

"Yes, overnight delivery would be perfect," she was saying. "We need them as soon as possible."

As she hung up, Becket admired her resolve. In just a few short days, she'd gone from a reluctant house-sitter to the town's Christmas savior.

"So," he said, wrapping his arms around her, pulling her against him. "What's the plan?"

Ruby leaned back into him, her voice filled with excitement. "What if we surprised the town? Do you think we could decorate while everyone's asleep, and they wake up to a winter wonderland?"

Becket raised an eyebrow. "So, you're suggesting a stealth operation? Sneak in under cover of darkness and transform the place overnight?"

Ruby grinned, even if he couldn't see it. "Do you think we can pull it off?"

"Pull it off?" He pressed a kiss to the top of her head. "I think we'll make the best midnight decorators this town has ever seen."

She gave a contented sigh, excitement humming between them. "It'll be like Christmas magic, but with more ladders and less Santa."

"Sounds like a plan," he said, already imagining how the town would react. "Just say the word, and I'll gather supplies and keep the goats occupied."

Ruby laughed, leaning up to kiss him again, her lips soft and sweet. "It's a deal. Let's make Aspen Cove sparkle."

CHAPTER SEVENTEEN

Ruby's fingers trembled with excitement as she signed for the delivery. The truck driver gave her a curious look as she practically bounced on her toes, but she couldn't contain her enthusiasm. The moment he drove away, she turned to Becket, her eyes sparkling.

"They're here!" she exclaimed, gesturing wildly at all the boxes. "Can you believe it? We did it!"

Becket's grin matched her own. "I still can't wrap my head around how fast this all came together," he said, shaking his head in amazement. "You're quite the miracle worker, Ruby."

A stirring rose in Ruby's chest at his words. It wasn't just the compliment—it was the way he said her name, like it was something that mattered. She pushed the feeling aside, focusing instead on the task in front of her.

As they unpacked string lights, garlands, wreaths, and an assortment of decorations, Ruby's mind buzzed with ideas. She pulled out a pair of life-sized nutcrackers, their painted faces grinning up at her. "Oh, these are perfect for Main Street!" she declared.

Becket hoisted a box of light-up reindeer. "And I know just where these can go. The kids will love them."

Ruby hesitated, her words catching in her throat. "I... I'm just trying to right a wrong," she admitted.

"The wrong my goats caused," Becket corrected with a grin. "I should've been the one to buy all this."

"It's a joint effort," she insisted. "You're paying in muscle and patience."

Ruby thought back to the day she arrived in Aspen Cove—determined to get in and get out, no strings attached. When had that changed? When had this place, these people, started to matter so much?

As the sun set, painting the sky in brilliant oranges and pinks, a surge of anticipation washed over Ruby. Soon, they'd be embarking on their secret mission to transform Aspen Cove overnight. The fading light cast long shadows across the snow-covered ground, and Ruby was mesmerized by the play of colors on the pristine white surface.

"Let's get some rest before tonight," Becket suggested, his hand resting on the small of her back. The touch sent a shiver up her spine.

Ruby nodded, though she doubted she'd be able to sleep a wink. "You're right. We've got a long night ahead of us."

A few hours later, under the cover of darkness, they set out. The snow had stopped falling, leaving behind a pristine blanket of white that glittered under the starlight. The night was clear, a canopy of stars twinkling above them like nature's own Christmas lights. Ruby tilted her head back, marveling at the vast expanse of the night sky. In the city, she'd never seen stars like this, so numerous and bright they seemed close enough to touch.

"Beautiful, isn't it?" Becket's voice was soft beside her.

"It's one of the things I love most about living in the mountains. You feel like you can see the entire universe."

Ruby nodded, unable to find words to express her awe. Just then, a streak of light flashed across the sky—a shooting star, brilliant and fleeting.

"Oh!" Ruby gasped, instinctively reaching for Becket's hand. "Did you see that?"

Becket squeezed her hand, his eyes wide with wonder. "I did. Quick, make a wish!"

Ruby closed her eyes, her heart full of the magic of the moment. She didn't wish for anything specific—how could she, when right now, everything seemed perfect? Instead, she wished for more moments like this, more nights under the stars with Becket by her side.

When she opened her eyes, she found Becket watching her. "What did you wish for?" he asked.

Ruby shook her head, a grin playing on her lips. "Can't tell you, or it won't come true. But maybe, if we're lucky, we'll see another one before the night is over."

Becket held onto her hand as they walked toward Ruby's rental car. "Well, I'd say we're already lucky. But I wouldn't mind a little extra star magic."

They approached the car, which was stuffed to the gills with decorations. Ruby laughed at the sight of garlands poking out of windows and a reindeer nose pressed against the back windshield.

"I still can't believe we managed to fit this much in here," she said, opening the driver's side door.

Becket grinned as he squeezed into the passenger seat. "It's like a Christmas clown car. I half-expect elves to start tumbling out."

They drove down the empty streets, the car groaning

under its burden. As they began unloading at the start of Main Street, Ruby realized the magnitude of their task.

"We're going to have to make a few trips back to the house," she said, her arms full of twinkling lights.

Becket nodded, already starting to untangle a stubborn strand. "Good thing we started early. We'll make it work."

And make it work they did. Over the next few hours, Ruby and Becket fell into a steady rhythm. They decorated a section of Main Street, then drove back to the house to reload the car with more supplies. Each trip became a mini adventure, filled with quiet laughter and a lighthearted competition to squeeze just one more box into the already overflowing vehicle.

By their third trip back, a sense of accomplishment settled over Ruby. "You know," she said as they pulled up to the curb, "I think I'm getting pretty good at this covert Christmas operation."

Becket reached over to tuck a loose strand of hair behind her ear. "Told you—you're a natural at spreading Christmas cheer."

As they resumed their work, Ruby kept glancing up at the sky, hoping to catch another glimpse of a shooting star. But even without one, the night felt alive with possibilities. The town was still, most residents long asleep. Ruby's heart pounded with a childlike excitement, as if she were sneaking downstairs on Christmas Eve.

They worked in easy silence, starting with Main Street. Ruby draped lush garlands along the storefronts, ensuring each one hung perfectly. Becket followed close behind, weaving twinkling lights through the greenery. The soft glow reflected off the snow, casting a magical shimmer across the street.

"These wreaths are gorgeous," Ruby whispered as she

hung one on the bakery door. Adorned with pinecones, berries, and a red velvet bow, the wreaths smelled like fresh pine.

Becket nodded as he wrestled a strand of lights around a lamppost. "The whole town's going to smell like Christmas."

He paused, his expression playful. "How long do you think it'll take Maisey to figure out it was us?" he asked as they festooned the diner window in greenery and plaid.

Ruby laughed, the sound echoing in the still night air. "Five minutes, tops. That woman has a sixth sense for town gossip."

As they worked their way down Main Street, Ruby placed the life-sized nutcrackers between businesses, positioning them as cheerful guardians. A grin spread across her face as she imagined the delight on children's faces when they saw them. "I used to be terrified of nutcrackers as a kid," she admitted.

Becket raised an eyebrow. "Really? The fearless Ruby, scared of nutcrackers?"

She stuck her tongue out at him playfully. "Hey, those teeth looked menacing to a six-year-old. What about you? Any childhood Christmas traumas I should know about?"

Becket pretended to think for a moment. "Well, there was that one year I caught my dad trying to eat Santa's cookies. Talk about childhood disillusionment."

Their laughter echoed through the empty street. Ruby noticed how easy it was to be with Becket, how natural their banter was. When had that happened?

"Hey, come help me with these," Becket said. He was setting up the light-up deer in the small park at the end of Main Street. Ruby hurried over, and together they arranged the deer in a graceful scene, as if they had just paused midleap. The twinkling lights on the deer seemed to dance, casting a soft glow on the surrounding snow.

As they worked, Ruby found her gaze continually drawn to Becket. The way his brow furrowed in concentration, the gentle strength in his hands as he adjusted the decorations, the way his eyes crinkled when he smiled at her.

The night wore on, and Ruby's initial burst of energy began to wane. She stifled a yawn as she hung the last of the wreaths on the sheriff's office door. The town hall clock chimed in the distance, reminding her of how long they'd been at it.

"Hey." Becket's voice was soft as he approached her. "Take a break. I've got this last bit." She started to protest, but Becket silenced her with a kiss. "You've been going non-stop for days. Rest for a bit."

Reluctantly, Ruby settled onto a nearby bench. She meant to close her eyes for just a moment, but the next thing she knew, Becket was gently shaking her awake.

"Ruby," he whispered, his breath warm against her ear. "Look."

She blinked awake, disoriented before gasping in awe. Main Street was transformed. Garlands draped across every storefront, twinkling with hundreds of tiny lights. Wreaths adorned each door, their red bows a cheerful contrast to the green. The lampposts were wrapped in lights and tinsel, glowing in the pre-dawn light.

The nutcrackers stood proudly between shops, and in the distance, she could see the light-up deer, looking as if they might come to life at any moment. The town's Christmas tree, which had been set up days ago, now looked even more majestic surrounded by the new decorations.

The entire scene was dusted with a light layer of frost, making everything sparkle as if touched by fairies.

"It's beautiful," she breathed, her eyes filling with tears. "Becket, it's perfect."

He pulled her close, and she nestled into his embrace, feeling safe and content. "We did it together," he whispered into her hair.

As they stood there, wrapped in each other's arms, a shift happened inside Ruby. This town, which had initially seemed like a burden, a reminder of loss, now felt like ... home. She thought of the laughter shared with Marge, the kindness of the townsfolk at the diner, the quiet moments with Becket and the goats.

Somewhere along the way, Aspen Cove had stolen her heart.

She thought back to her first day here, how cold and unwelcoming the town had seemed. Now, looking at the twinkling lights and decorations, she saw it through new eyes. It wasn't just the physical transformation of the town that struck her, but how she herself had changed. The Ruby who arrived in Aspen Cove weeks ago would never have imagined feeling this sense of belonging, this connection to a place and its people.

"What are you thinking?" Becket asked, his thumb wiping away a tear she hadn't realized had fallen.

Ruby looked up at him, seeing her future reflected in his eyes. "I'm thinking that I don't want this to end," she admitted. "Being here, with you, in this town ... it feels right. It's like I've found a piece of myself I didn't know was missing."

Becket's face lit up, brighter than all the Christmas lights combined. He leaned down, capturing her lips in a kiss that made her toes curl. When they parted, both breathless, Ruby laughed, the sound bubbling up with pure joy.

"What's so funny?" Becket asked, his eyes twinkling with amusement.

"Just thinking about how much has changed," Ruby replied, shaking her head in wonder. "I came here dreading every moment, and now ... it's like this place has worked some kind of Christmas magic on me. On us."

As the first rays of sunlight began to peek over the horizon, Ruby and Becket drove home in comfortable silence. Becket steered the car with one hand while the other rested over Ruby's, their fingers intertwined. When they reached the driveway, he quickly hopped out and raced around to open her door, ever the gentleman. Ruby stepped out, and their hands naturally found each other again.

The crisp morning air nipped at their cheeks as they strolled toward the house, but warmth spread through Ruby, a glow of contentment settling deep in her chest. The sky had shifted from inky black to a soft lavender, with streaks of pink and gold announcing the coming day. It seemed symbolic somehow, like the dawn of a new chapter in her life.

They climbed onto the porch, and Becket pulled her close, his strong arms encircling her waist. "I can't wait until everyone sees what we did," he whispered, his breath warm against her ear, the excitement clear in his voice.

Ruby nodded, excitement bubbling in her chest. "Me too..." She turned in his arms, reaching up to cradle his face in her hands. "Thank you for everything. Especially all the kisses."

"You like my kisses?"

"They're the best I've ever had."

"Well then," Becket said, pulling her closer, "we shouldn't waste a single minute doing anything but kissing."

Their lips met again, but this time the kiss was different.

Deeper, more urgent. All the emotions of the night—the excitement, the joy, the newfound affection—seemed to pour into it. Ruby's hands slid into Becket's hair as he pulled her flush against him, erasing any space between them.

They stumbled through the front door, neither willing to break the kiss. Ruby shrugged out of her coat, letting it fall to the floor with a soft thump. Becket followed suit, his coat joining hers in a heap. Their hands roamed, exploring, as if trying to memorize every curve and plane of each other's bodies. The sudden heat of the house contrasted sharply with the chill still clinging to their skin, adding to the intensity of their touches.

Ruby's hands found Becket's, and she began tugging him towards the bedroom, her intentions clear in her eyes. Becket hesitated, his voice husky with desire but tinged with concern. "Ruby, are you sure about this? About us?"

In response, Ruby pulled him down for another searing kiss. When they parted, she met his gaze, her eyes filled with certainty and want. "I've never been surer of anything in my life," she whispered against his lips. "I want you, Becket. All of you."

They stumbled into the bedroom, leaving a trail of discarded clothing behind them. As they collapsed onto the bed, Ruby marveled at the sensation of Becket's skin against hers. Each touch, each caress sent electric sparks through her body.

Their lovemaking was both tender and passionate, a perfect reflection of their journey together. Ruby lost herself in the sensation, in the feeling of Becket's hands on her body, his lips on her skin. She poured all of her emotions into every touch, every kiss, wanting Becket to feel how much he meant to her.

As they moved together, it seemed to Ruby that her heart might burst with the intensity of her feelings. She saw the same emotions reflected in Becket's eyes—affection, wonder, and a hint of awe, as if he couldn't quite believe this was real.

Afterwards, they lay tangled together, Ruby's head resting on Becket's chest as he traced lazy patterns on her back. The morning sun filtered through the curtains, bathing them in a soft, golden light. Outside, they could hear the town beginning to stir, the distant sounds of early risers discovering their handiwork.

A swell of emotion rose in Ruby's chest, filling her entire being. She tilted her head up, meeting Becket's gaze. "You know," she said, wonder in her voice, "I think I could fall in love with you."

Becket's hand stilled, and Ruby held her breath, worried she'd said too much. Then his face broke into a tender smile, his eyes shining with affection. He leaned down, pressing a gentle kiss to her forehead. "I think I could fall in love with you too," he whispered against her skin.

The admission hung in the air between them, full of promise and possibility. It wasn't a declaration of love, not yet, but it was a step towards something deep and meaningful. Ruby snuggled closer to Becket, feeling safe and cherished in his arms.

As they drifted off to sleep, wrapped in each other's embrace, a deep sense of peace settled over Ruby. Her last thought before sleep claimed her was how their mission to carefully replace the decorations of Aspen Cove hadn't just brightened the town—it had transformed her heart as well.

CHAPTER EIGHTEEN

Becket woke, his arms still wrapped around Ruby's warm body. Sunlight streamed through the curtains, casting a golden glow across the rumpled sheets. Blinking away the last remnants of sleep, he savored the memories of their passionate morning.

Ruby stirred against him, her eyes fluttering open. A wave of contentment settled over her as she met his gaze. "Good morning," she said, her voice still husky with sleep.

"I think it might be closer to good afternoon," Becket glanced at the clock on the nightstand. It read 12:17 PM.

As if on cue, Ruby's stomach growled loudly, causing them both to burst into laughter.

"I guess that's what happens when you skip breakfast," Ruby said, a hint of a blush coloring her cheeks.

Becket's own stomach rumbled in response. "Looks like we worked up quite an appetite," he said. "What do you say we head to Maisey's for some much-needed sustenance?"

Ruby stretched languidly, then nodded. "I'm so hungry I could eat a horse ... or maybe one of your goats," she teased.

"Hey now," Becket said with a smirk. "Those goats are practically family. But Maisey's pancakes? They'll make you forget you ever considered livestock."

They reluctantly disentangled themselves from each other and the warm cocoon of blankets. As they got dressed, their eyes met in brief, playful glances. This thing between them was new and exciting, but it also felt surprisingly comfortable, like coming home.

"Ready to face the day?" he asked, offering his hand to Ruby as they headed for the door.

"As long as there's food involved, absolutely," she replied, lacing her fingers through his.

Together, they stepped out into the crisp afternoon air, the events of the morning having deepened their connection in ways neither had anticipated.

The walk to Maisey's was quick, their growling stomachs spurring them on. As they strolled down Main Street, they admired their handiwork from the night before. The garlands swayed in the breeze, and ornaments caught the winter sun, transforming Aspen Cove into a magical Christmas wonderland.

"It does look magical," Ruby said, her eyes bright as she took in the scene. "I can't believe we did all this in one night."

Becket grinned, giving her hand a squeeze. "We make quite a team, don't we?"

As they entered Maisey's, the cheerful tinkling of the bell above the door announced their arrival. The familiar scent of coffee and bacon enveloped them, and Becket noticed Ruby relax beside him. Through the diner's large front windows, they could see their decorations.

"Well, look who decided to join the land of the living," Maisey called out from behind the counter, her eyes twinkling with amusement. "I was beginning to think you two had hibernated for the winter."

Becket's cheeks heated up, and a quick glance at Ruby showed she was blushing too. 'We, uh, had a late night,' he mumbled, guiding Ruby to a booth near the window.

"I bet you did," Maisey winked, following them with menus in hand. "What with all that sneaking around and decorating the town."

Becket and Ruby exchanged startled looks. "How did you—"

"Oh, honey," Maisey said, "in a town this size, news travels faster than you can say 'Christmas spirit.' Sheriff Cooper's security cameras caught you red-handed."

Becket groaned, burying his face in his hands. "So much for our covert operation."

"Are we in trouble?" Ruby asked, her voice tinged with worry.

Maisey's laugh rang out, drawing the attention of the other diners. "Trouble? Darlin', you two are the talk of the town! Everyone's buzzing about how this will be the best Christmas Aspen Cove has seen in years."

Emotion surged through Becket, her words hitting harder than he expected. Beside him, Ruby squeezed his hand, her eyes shining with relief and joy.

They ordered a feast fit for, well, two hungry people who'd skipped breakfast. As they waited for their food, the diner's door chimed again, and Katie from the bakery bustled in, her cheeks rosy from the cold.

"Oh good, you're here!" she said, spotting them. She hurried over, practically vibrating with excitement. "I've been looking all over for you two. I wanted to thank you for the decorations—they're absolutely perfect! And I wanted to make sure you're both ready for the cookie exchange tomorrow night."

Ruby looked at Becket, a question in her eyes. Becket turned to Katie. "We'll be there. I'm planning to make my gingerbread cookies. They're always a hit."

Katie clapped her hands in delight. "Oh, that's wonderful! You know, everything's coming together so nicely for the festival. Doc's even agreed to dress up as Santa for the tree lighting ceremony. The one thing we're missing is the reindeer!"

She glanced at her watch and her eyes widened. "Oh, I've got to run! I just wanted to say hello and thanks. I've got loads of brownie batter to make for tomorrow night. See you both then!"

With a quick wave, Katie hurried out of the diner, the bell chiming again as the door closed behind her.

Their food arrived, and they dug in with gusto. Between bites of syrupy pancakes and crispy bacon, Ruby glanced at Becket. "So, tell me about these gingerbread cookies of yours. Are they that special?"

Becket grinned, leaning in conspiratorially. "Well, if you must know, it's an old family recipe. Been passed down for generations, and I'll have you know it's won the unofficial 'Best Cookie' title three years running at my mom's church social."

Ruby raised an eyebrow. "Is that so? Sounds like I might have some competition then."

"Oh?" Becket leaned back, crossing his arms. "Planning on dethroning the cookie king, are you?"

She shrugged. "Maybe. I guess you'll just have to wait and see."

As they finished their meal, Becket marveled at how natural this all seemed—sharing a meal, teasing each other, making plans for the day. It was as if Ruby had always been a part of his life here in Aspen Cove.

After settling the bill, and enduring more good-natured teasing from Maisey, they headed out.

"We should stop at the Corner Store for the cookie ingredients," Becket suggested. "I don't think you have everything we need at your place."

Ruby nodded in agreement. "Good thinking."

They made a quick stop at the Corner Store, picking up flour, molasses, and the special blend of spices Becket's grandmother always used in her gingerbread recipe. As they approached Ruby's house, bags in hand, Becket's gaze drifted toward the garage, already thinking ahead to their next task—checking on the goats.

"Let's put these groceries inside and then check on the goats," Ruby suggested. "They could use some fresh air."

After depositing the bags in the kitchen, they headed to the garage. Becket opened the side door, greeted by the soft bleating of the goats.

"Hey there," he said, giving each a gentle pat. "How about we get you outside for a bit?"

Together, Becket and Ruby led the goats to the backyard. As they watched the animals graze and frolic in the open space, Katie's words about the missing reindeer echoed in Becket's mind, sparking an idea.

"Hey," he said, turning to Ruby with a grin, "what would you say to adding a little extra flair to the tree lighting ceremony?"

She eyed him suspiciously. "What kind of flair are we talking about?"

He gestured toward the goats, who were wandering around aimlessly. "How about some four-legged reindeer stand-ins?"

Ruby's eyes widened, then crinkled with laughter. "Are you suggesting we dress up your goats for the ceremony?"

"Why not?" Becket shrugged. "It'll add to the atmosphere. Plus, I bet the children would love it."

"You're crazy," Ruby said, shaking her head. But her eyes were sparkling with amusement. "But I love it. Let's do it."

They spent the next hour selecting the most docile goats and brainstorming costume ideas. In the end, they decided on simple reindeer antlers and red harnesses with jingle bells that they could overnight from Amazon.

"I know we haven't met Mrs. Brown yet, but we should ask if she'd be willing to knit some scarves for them," Ruby suggested as they headed back inside. "That would complete the look, you know?"

Becket nodded, feeling a sense of excitement at her enthusiasm. "That's a great idea. We can stop by her place later this afternoon."

Back in the kitchen, they started gathering the ingredients for their cookie-baking session. Just as they were about to begin, Ruby's phone rang. It was Marge. She answered, putting it on speaker so Becket could hear too.

"Ruby, you won't believe this!" Marge's excited voice filled the kitchen. "A couple came through town this morning and absolutely fell in love with all the Christmas decorations and the whole holiday atmosphere. They want to buy a winter home here in Aspen Cove, calling it their 'little piece of Christmas heaven.'"

Ruby's eyes widened. "That's wonderful for the town, but what does that have to do with me?"

"Well," Marge continued, "they want to buy your uncle's house. They're ready to make an offer."

Becket and Ruby exchanged surprised looks. "But they haven't even seen the house," Ruby said.

"They don't care what it looks like, dear," Marge explained. "They plan to gut the place and rebuild anyway. They just want the location."

Ruby fell silent, her expression caught between emotions. Becket could see the conflict in her eyes.

"The offer they're making..." Marge hesitated, then continued, "It's substantially more than what I would have suggested as a listing price, Ruby. It's a fantastic deal."

Ruby nodded, even though Marge couldn't see her. "I ... I need some time to think about it. Can I let you know tomorrow?"

"Of course. Take your time. I'll be waiting to hear from you."

After they hung up, Ruby leaned against the counter, her face pensive. Becket approached her cautiously.

"Hey," he said. "Are you okay?"

Ruby looked up at him, her eyes shimmering with unshed tears. "It's just ... the money is what I came here for. It would solve so many problems. But the idea of them tearing down Uncle Peter's house, erasing him ... it hurts more than I expected."

Becket pulled her into a gentle hug. "I understand. It's a big decision. You don't have to make it right now."

Ruby nodded against his chest. "One day at a time, right?"

"One day at a time," Becket agreed, holding her close.

They stood in silence, the weight of the unexpected news hanging between them. Emotions swirled in Becket's chest—concern for Ruby, a selfish hope that she might stay, and guilt for even thinking about his own desires in this moment.

"Time to get started on those cookies," Becket said, breaking the tension. "Baking always helps me clear my head. Maybe it'll do the same for you?"

Ruby nodded, seemingly grateful for the distraction. "You're right. Let's do it."

They spent the next few hours in a flurry of measuring, mixing, and playful flour-flicking. Becket showed Ruby the intricacies of his grandmother's gingerbread recipe, while she introduced him to a few tricks she'd picked up from watching baking shows. The familiar motions of baking seemed to soothe Ruby, and soon they were laughing and joking as they worked.

By the time they had several batches of gingerbread cookies chilling in the fridge, they were both covered in a fine dusting of flour and sugar. The kitchen was warm and fragrant with the scent of spices and molasses.

"I think," Ruby said, wiping a smear of flour from Becket's cheek, "that we'd better clean up before we go see Mrs. Brown. We look like we've been wrestling in a bakery."

Becket caught her hand, pressing a soft kiss to her palm. "I don't know, I think the flour suits you. You look like a Christmas angel."

Ruby laughed, the sound warming Becket's heart. It was good to see her happy again after the news from Marge.

After quick showers and changes of clothes, they flipped through the old phone book on Ruby's counter, scanning the names. Sure enough, there was only one Brown listed. "That must be her," Ruby said with a nod.

With the address in hand, they headed out to Mrs. Brown's cozy cottage, ready to make their introduction.

The elderly woman was delighted by their request for goat-sized scarves and immediately set to work, shooing them away with promises to have them ready before the tree lighting the next evening.

As they walked back to Ruby's place, hand in hand, Ruby said quietly, "You know, I've never been so welcomed in a place before. It's like everyone here genuinely cares."

Becket squeezed her hand. "That's Aspen Cove for you. Once you're here, you're family."

She didn't respond, but he saw something in her eyes—wonder and, perhaps, a touch of longing. He wanted to ask her about the house, about her decision, but he held back. She would talk when she was ready.

They spent the rest of the afternoon and evening decorating the cookies they'd baked earlier, filling the kitchen with laughter and the sweet scent of sugar and spices.

CHAPTER NINETEEN

The next day, Ruby stood in the kitchen, watching Becket as he iced the gingerbread cookies. His brow was furrowed in concentration, the tip of his tongue poking out as he piped intricate designs onto each gingerbread man. The sight would have been endearing if Ruby's mind wasn't still preoccupied with Marge's phone call from yesterday.

"I think I need some air," Ruby said, causing Becket to look up from his work. "I'm just going to take a quick walk, clear my head a bit."

Concern crossed Becket's face. "Do you want me to come with you?"

Ruby shook her head. "No, you stay here and work your cookie magic. I won't be long."

Before Becket could protest, Ruby grabbed her coat and headed out the door. The crisp winter air nipped at her cheeks as she made her way down the snow-dusted sidewalk. Her mind was a whirlwind of conflicting thoughts and emotions.

The offer on the house was more than she could have hoped for. It would solve so many of her problems—pay off her debts, give her a fresh start. Isn't that why she came to Aspen Cove in the first place? To sell the house and move on with her life?

But as she walked past the twinkling lights and decorations lining Main Street, a pang hit Ruby's chest. This town, which had seemed so foreign and unwelcoming when she first arrived, now was home. The thought of leaving it all behind made her heart ache in a way she hadn't expected.

Lost in thought, Ruby almost bumped into someone coming out of B's Bakery.

"Oh! I'm so sorry," Ruby apologized, steadying herself.

"No harm done," came the cheerful reply. Ruby looked up to see Katie, the baker, balancing a tray of steaming muffins. "Ruby! Care to be my taste tester?"

Before Ruby could respond, Katie was ushering her into the warm, sweet-smelling bakery. "I'm trying out a new recipe for the Christmas festival. I want to serve something other than brownies. These are gingerbread muffins with eggnog glaze. What do you think?"

Ruby was perched on a chair in front of the window, a muffin in hand before she could process what was happening. She took a bite, the flavors of spice and sweetness exploding on her tongue.

"This is amazing," she said, genuinely impressed.

Katie beamed. "Oh, I'm so glad you like it! I was worried the eggnog might be too much, but Bowie insisted it was perfect."

As if summoned by his name, Bowie appeared from the back room, holding his daughter Sahara's hand. "Hey there, Ruby," he greeted. "Enjoying Katie's latest creation?"

Ruby nodded, swallowing another bite of muffin. "It's delicious. You've got a real talent, Katie."

Katie nodded. "Thank you. You know, baking wasn't

always my plan. Life has a funny way of leading you where you're meant to be."

There was something in Katie's tone that piqued Ruby's curiosity. "What do you mean?"

Katie exchanged a glance with Bowie, who nodded encouragingly. "Well, it's quite a story. Do you have some time?"

Ruby thought about the decision waiting for her back at the house, about Becket and the cookies. But something told her this was important. She nodded.

Katie took a deep breath. "Before I came here, I was living in Dallas. I had a corporate job, the kind where you wear uncomfortable shoes and count down the minutes until you can leave. I thought that was what I wanted, you know? The big city life, the career."

Ruby nodded, the description hitting close to home.

"But then," Katie continued, her voice softening, "I got sick. Really sick. It turned out I needed a heart transplant."

Ruby's eyes widened. "Oh, Katie, I'm so sorry."

Katie reached out to squeeze Ruby's hand. "Don't be. It led me here, to this life I never knew I wanted." She paused, her eyes growing distant, as if reliving a memory. "A few years after the transplant, I received a pink letter. It was from a woman named Bea Bennett, who is someone I'd never met. The letter ... it changed everything."

"What did it say?" Ruby asked, captivated.

Katie laughed. "It was the strangest thing. Bea had given me this bakery and had written me a list of 100 reasons why I would be wonderful in this little town called Aspen Cove, a place I'd never even heard of before."

"A hundred reasons?" Ruby echoed, amazed.

"Yes, and the first reason on that list was 'because you have a good heart.'" Katie's hand unconsciously moved to her chest. "It wasn't just a list, though. Somehow, Bea knew everything about me. My hopes, my fears, even the dreams I'd been too afraid to admit to myself."

A chill ran down Ruby's spine. "That's incredible. But how did she know all that about you?"

Katie's expression turned bittersweet. "It turns out, the heart I received … it was from Bea's daughter, Brandy. Bea had hired a private investigator to find out about me. She wanted to know who had received her daughter's heart."

Ruby's hand flew to her mouth. "Oh, Katie…"

Katie nodded. "It was overwhelming at first. But Bea's letter felt like a gift. Not just a list of reasons, but a roadmap to a life I didn't even know I wanted. So, I decided to take a chance. I came to Aspen Cove."

"And that's where you met Bowie?" Ruby asked.

Katie's face lit up. "Yes. He was one of the first people I met here. We just … clicked. And the rest of the town… Ruby, from the moment I arrived, it was like coming home. Everyone rallied around me, helped me reopen the bakery. They became my extended family, gave me a second chance at life."

Ruby nodded, thinking about her own experiences in Aspen Cove. The kindness of the townspeople, the way they'd embraced her and Becket, goats and all.

"I know you're facing a big decision," Katie said. "Marge mentioned the offer on your uncle's house. And I'm not trying to sway you one way or the other. But I want you to know that whatever you choose, you have a place here. In Aspen Cove, no one's ever truly alone."

Ruby's eyes filled with tears. "Thank you, Katie. That means more than you know."

As Ruby left the bakery, her mind was even more conflicted than before. But now, mixed in with the uncertainty, was a feeling she couldn't quite explain. She thought about Katie's story, about the mysterious Bea Bennett and the power of a pink letter to change a life.

Almost without realizing it, Ruby ended up outside Maisey's Diner. The warm glow from the windows beckoned her inside, promising comfort and clarity.

The bell above the door jingled as Ruby entered, drawing Maisey's attention from behind the counter.

"Well, look who it is," Maisey said, her eyes twinkling. "Shouldn't you be elbow-deep in cookie dough right about now?"

Ruby managed a weak smile as she slid onto a stool at the counter. "I needed a break. Some time to think."

Maisey's expression softened. She poured a cup of coffee and placed it in front of Ruby without being asked. "When Marge came by for coffee this morning, she told me about the offer on the house. That's quite a decision you've got in front of you."

Ruby wrapped her hands around the warm mug, grateful for its comforting heat. Marge sure got around—nothing stayed quiet for long in this town. "I don't know what to do, Maisey. The money would solve so many problems, but..."

"But you're not sure if it's worth giving up everything else," Maisey finished for her.

Ruby nodded, surprised at how easily Maisey had read her thoughts. "Is it crazy to even hesitate? I mean, this is what I came here for. To sell the house and go back to my life in Chicago."

Maisey leaned on the counter, her eyes filled with understanding. "You know, Ruby, your situation reminds me of something I went through years ago. Mind if I share a little story?"

Ruby took a sip of her coffee, settling in to listen.

"It was about thirty years ago," Maisey began. "I was a single mom, struggling to make ends meet in the city. I came back to Aspen Cove because I had nowhere else to go. This diner was up for sale, and I knew it could be a fresh start for me and my son, Dalton, but I didn't have two pennies to rub together."

Ruby leaned forward, intrigued.

"That's when Doc stepped in," Maisey continued. "He loaned me the money to buy this place. Said he believed in me, and that Aspen Cove needed a good diner. It wasn't easy at first, juggling a new business and a young kid, but the town rallied around us. They became our family."

Maisey paused, refilling Ruby's coffee cup before continuing. "I had to make a choice back then—between the life I thought I wanted in the city and the one waiting for me here. Not just the diner, but the kind of life I wanted for myself and my son."

Ruby nodded, her chest tightening. "I never thought I'd feel so torn about this. When I first got here, all I wanted was to sell the house and leave. But now..."

"Now you've gotten a taste of what Aspen Cove has to offer," Maisey finished for her. "The sense of community, the way everyone looks out for each other. Not to mention a certain handsome goat farmer."

Ruby's cheeks flushed at the mention of Becket. "He's part of it too," she admitted. "I can't imagine not having him in my life now."

Maisey reached out and patted Ruby's hand. "Listen, honey. You need to figure out what kind of life you're looking for. If it's fast-paced city living you want, then maybe Aspen Cove isn't the place for you. But if it's a life with that goat herder of yours, well … I'm sure the city isn't too keen on having goats roaming around."

Ruby laughed at that, picturing Houdini trying to navigate a Chicago sidewalk.

"There's no right or wrong answer here," Maisey continued. "You've got to do what feels right for you. But don't make this decision based solely on the money. Consider what you'd be gaining or giving up, too."

Ruby took a deep breath, feeling some of the tension leave her body. "Thank you, Maisey. You've given me a lot to think about."

As Ruby stood to leave, Maisey called out, "Whatever you decide, we'll understand, and we'll be here for you."

The words warmed Ruby's heart as she stepped back out into the cold night air. Her mind was still swirling with thoughts, but now there was a glimmer of clarity among the confusion.

She made her way back to Uncle Peter's house, her steps slow and thoughtful. There was a sense of togetherness and community that seemed to permeate every corner of Aspen Cove. She thought about Becket, about the goats, about the unexpected joy she'd found here.

By the time Ruby reached the front porch, she knew she wasn't ready to decide yet. There was still so much to consider, so much she wasn't sure about. But for the first time since receiving the offer, she finally had the space to truly weigh her options.

As she opened the door, the scent of gingerbread enveloped her. Becket looked up from his icing work.

"Hey," he said. "Feeling better?"

Ruby nodded, moving to stand beside him at the kitchen counter. "A little. I've got a lot to think about, but talking to Katie and Maisey helped."

Becket's eyes searched hers, concern evident in his expression. "Yeah? Want to talk about it?"

Ruby shook her head. "Not just yet. I think I need to let things settle a bit first. But thank you. For being here, for understanding."

Becket nodded, respecting her need for space. "Whenever you're ready, I'm here to listen."

Ruby leaned in, pressing a soft kiss to his cheek. "I know. Now, how about you teach me the secret to your award-winning gingerbread decorating?"

As they worked side by side, laughing and teasing each other, some of the weight lifted from Ruby's shoulders. She knew she had a big decision ahead of her, but for now, she was content to live in the moment. The future, with all its uncertainties and possibilities, could wait until tomorrow.

CHAPTER TWENTY

The pale winter sun had only just risen when Becket stirred, the familiar sounds of bleating goats rousing him from sleep. He glanced over at Ruby, still peacefully slumbering, her hair splayed across the pillow. He allowed himself to imagine waking up like this every morning, in this house, with Ruby by his side.

Shaking off the thought, Becket quietly slipped out of bed and made his way to the garage. Inside, he found Daisy where they'd left her the night before, nestled comfortably in her corner on a bed of hay.

"Morning, mama," he said, kneeling beside her. Daisy lifted her head, acknowledging him with a gentle bleat. Becket ran his hand along her side, feeling the slight movements of the kid within. "Not today, huh? Well, that's okay. You take your time."

He spent the next hour tending to the goats, his mind wandering to the day ahead. The Christmas cookie festival and tree lighting loomed large in Becket's mind. He was excited about experiencing it for the first time alongside

Ruby. Maybe they could both find a sense of home in this town.

By the time he returned to the house, the smell of coffee filled the air. He found Ruby in the kitchen, hair tousled from sleep, clutching a steaming mug.

"There you are," she said, smiling as she handed him a cup. "How's our mama-to-be?"

Becket accepted the coffee gratefully. "Content as can be. I don't think we'll be seeing any kids today, but you never know with goats. They like to keep you on your toes."

Ruby's laugh was warm, heating Becket more than the coffee ever could. "Kind of like a certain goat herder I know," she teased.

They spent the morning sorting through more of Uncle Peter's boxes, laughing at the odd knick-knacks and marveling at the eclectic collection. Becket watched Ruby as she examined each item, her expression alternating between amusement and thoughtfulness.

"What do you think Uncle Peter was doing with a collection of vintage potato mashers?" Ruby asked, holding up an ornate specimen.

Becket grinned, taking the masher and turning it over in his hands. "Maybe he was preparing for a mashed potato apocalypse? You never know when you might need to whip up a batch in a hurry."

Ruby's laughter filled the room, and Becket's heart swelled. He loved the way her eyes crinkled at the corners when she let go and laughed.

As they worked, Becket noticed how at ease Ruby seemed, how her laughter came more freely with each passing day—a far cry from the stressed, overwhelmed woman who had arrived in Aspen Cove just a short time ago.

They unearthed a box of old Christmas ornaments, each one wrapped in yellowed newspaper. Ruby held up a delicate glass bauble, its surface painted with a snowy scene.

"These are beautiful," she said, turning the ornament to catch the light. "I wonder what kind of Christmases Uncle Peter had here."

Becket moved closer, peering at the decoration. "I bet they were something special. Maybe we could use some of these on the tree this year?" He paused, realizing what he'd said. "I mean, if you're planning to stay that long."

Ruby's expression softened, but before she could respond, Becket's stomach let out a loud growl. They both burst out laughing, the moment broken.

"I think that's our cue for lunch," Ruby said, setting the ornament back in its box.

As they prepared sandwiches, Becket's mind raced. He wanted to ask Ruby about her plans, about whether she was still thinking of selling the house and returning to Chicago. But he held back, not wanting to pressure her.

It was nearing mid-afternoon when Becket realized they were out of the small candies he used for decorating the gingerbread cookies. "I need to run into town," he said, glancing at his watch. "We're out of those little candies I used for the buttons."

"Oh, I can go," Ruby offered, but Becket shook his head.

"No, you stay here and keep sorting. I won't be long."

Becket needed a voice of reason when it came to his feelings for Ruby, and if anyone had wisdom to offer, it was Doc Parker. The man was practically the town's historian— oldest in years and, likely, wisest in words.

In town, Becket found the candies he needed at the

Corner Store. As he was leaving, he noticed it was nearing four o'clock—Doc's usual time for a pint at Bishop's Brewhouse. On impulse, he headed over.

The warm, hoppy smell of the brewery enveloped Becket as he entered. He found Doc at the bar, already nursing a pint.

"Well, if it isn't our resident goat whisperer," Doc said. "Pull up a stool, son."

Becket sat down and ordered a beer, already feeling a bit lighter in the company of Doc. "Thanks, Doc. I was hoping to catch you. I need some advice."

Doc raised an eyebrow, his eyes twinkling with amusement. "Advice, huh? That's gonna cost you."

Becket's lips twitched. "Like a copay?"

Doc shook his head. "No, son. You either buy my next beer—because I'm gonna need it when the kids start climbing on my lap—or you play me a game of tic-tac-toe." He nodded toward a grid already drawn up on a napkin on the bar, as if it was just waiting for a challenger. "But I should warn you ... I never lose."

Becket shook his head, grinning. "So, I'm buying the beer either way, huh?"

Doc leaned back, a satisfied look on his face. "Maybe. But it's cheaper than a copay. Could be your lucky day. Now tell me what's on your mind."

Becket took a breath, fiddling with the edges of the napkin grid. "It's Ruby," he confessed. "I want her to stay, more than anything. But I don't have any right to ask her to. I mean, it's not even my house she's trying to figure out. I don't want to be the guy who makes her feel like she has to choose me over everything she's got waiting back in Chicago."

Doc placed an O on the napkin, the pencil scratching against the paper as he leaned in. "You know, son, Ruby seems like a smart woman. From what I hear, she already got an offer sight unseen, didn't she?"

Becket nodded, still staring at the tic-tac-toe board. "Yeah. Could've signed the papers, been done with it."

"But she didn't," Doc said with a knowing nod. "She's stalling, isn't she? Did you ever wonder why?"

Becket looked up, meeting Doc's steady gaze. "Yeah, I do."

"That's because she's figuring out what's important, where she fits. Ruby seems like the kind of girl who appreciates family, history. If all she wanted was a quick buck, she would have signed those sale papers and flown back to Chicago already. It sounds to me like she's trying to find out if Aspen Cove could be home. If it feels like a place she could put down roots."

Doc's words hit home. "So ... what do I do?" Becket ran a hand through his hair, his frustration clear. "Doc, I've got nothing to offer her. I've got a beat-up truck and some goats. Not a solid foundation to build a future on."

Doc chuckled, the sound deep and rich like the bark of an old tree. "Let me tell you something about love, Becket. Ain't no bank account big enough, no fancy car fast enough, no house grand enough that can hold a candle to the feeling of loving and being loved. Real love ... well, it doesn't care if you're driving a shiny new car or a rusted truck that needs a prayer to start each morning."

Becket stayed silent, his eyes fixed on Doc, waiting for the lesson he knew was coming.

"I've seen men with million-dollar deals and big city dreams who still went to bed lonely every night," Doc continued, his voice softening with a touch of nostalgia.

"And I've seen others with nothing but a roof over their heads and a woman who'd stand by their side through thick and thin, and they lived richer lives than most folks could ever dream. You see, love isn't about what you can put on paper, Becket. It's about what you can put in someone's heart."

Becket swallowed, absorbing the words. "But what if she wants more than that?"

Doc leaned forward, tapping the table with his finger to make sure he had Becket's full attention. "Then let her go after it. Let her figure out if all that glitters is gold. But if she's stalling, if she's hesitating on that offer for the house, then maybe—just maybe—she's finding out that real gold's right here in Aspen Cove. And you, my boy, might just be worth more than any sight-unseen offer she's got."

Becket's lips twitched, and something stirred in his chest. "You make it sound simple."

Doc grinned back, a twinkle in his eye. "Love is simple, son. It's folks that make it complicated. So, let her make her choice, but in the meantime, show her that your beat-up truck and goats aren't just things—they're part of a life that she could love."

Becket nodded, feeling the truth in the words. "I guess I've got some showing to do."

Doc clapped him on the back. "That's right. Now, let's finish this game. And remember, it could still be your lucky day."

When Becket returned home, he checked on Daisy again before heading into the house. She seemed comfortable, showing no signs of impending labor. He made a mental note to check on her again before they left for the tree lighting and cookie exchange.

He found Ruby in the kitchen, making a fresh pot of coffee.

"Hey," he said, not wanting to startle her. "Ready for tonight?"

Ruby looked up. "As ready as we'll ever be. Did you get the candies?"

Becket held up the bag triumphantly. "Mission accomplished. Now, let's turn these cookies into little works of art."

As they worked side by side, decorating the cookies, Becket couldn't stop glancing at Ruby. The way she bit her lip in concentration as she piped icing, the small, pleased smile when a design turned out perfectly—he wanted to remember every detail.

As the day wore on, they turned their attention to the two goats they'd decided to bring to the tree lighting ceremony. Becket had chosen to leave Daisy at home due to her pregnancy, opting instead for the enthusiastic Sir Chomps-a-Lot and Houdini. As for Houdini, leaving him behind seemed riskier than bringing him along—who knew what trouble he might get into if left unsupervised?

Dressing them proved to be a challenge, with Houdini living up to his namesake.

"Come on, you little troublemaker," Becket grunted, struggling to fasten a pair of felt antlers onto Houdini's head. The goat bleated indignantly, twisting his neck to avoid the offending accessory. "It's just for a few hours. You can handle it."

Ruby watched. "You know," she said, "I never thought I'd see the day when dressing up goats for a tree lighting would be a normal part of my life."

Just as they were trying to figure out how to make the goats look more festive, there was a knock at the front door.

"I'll get it," Ruby said, hurrying through the door that led from the garage into the house.

Becket continued wrestling with Houdini's antlers, only looking up when he heard Ruby return. She and Mrs. Brown entered. Mrs. Brown's cat Mr. Piddles cradled in one arm and a bag of knitted items in the other. Becket had to stifle a laugh when he saw Mr. Piddles dressed in a full elf costume, complete with pointy hat and shoes. The cat's expression could be described as one of utter resignation.

"Good evening," Mrs. Brown chirped. "I've brought those scarves for your goats."

"Oh, Mrs. Brown, thank you so much," Ruby said, her voice warm with gratitude. "We were just getting the goats ready."

Becket caught Ruby's eye and mouthed, "Poor cat," as he struggled to keep his laughter in check, causing Ruby to stifle a giggle.

They spent the next few minutes wrangling the goats into their new scarves, with Houdini doing his best to eat Mr. Piddles' elf hat. The cat, for his part, maintained a dignified air of long-suffering patience.

As Mrs. Brown prepared to leave, she turned to Ruby and Becket. "You two make such a lovely couple," she said, her eyes twinkling. "It's so nice to see young love blossoming in Aspen Cove."

Becket's cheeks heated up, and he saw Ruby's face turn a delightful shade of pink. Before either of them could say a thing, she was out the door, Mr. Piddles in tow.

An awkward silence fell between them, broken by Houdini's attempt to eat his own scarf.

"Well," Becket said, clearing his throat, "time to head out. Don't want to be late for the big event."

Ruby nodded, still looking a bit flustered. "Right. Yes. The tree lighting."

As they headed out, Becket made one last check on Daisy. Satisfied that she was comfortable and showing no signs of imminent labor, he joined Ruby and the goats outside.

The crisp evening air nipped at their cheeks as they headed into town, Houdini and Sir Chomps-a-Lot trotting beside them on leashes. The streets were alive with activity, holiday music drifting through the air, accompanied by the scent of cinnamon and pine needles from every direction.

"It's like something out of a Hallmark movie," Ruby marveled, taking in the twinkling lights and cheerful decorations they had installed.

Becket grinned, pulling Houdini back as the goat eyed a wreath like a salad buffet. "They say Aspen Cove doesn't do anything halfway when it comes to Christmas."

Ruby's eyes lit up at that. "I've never seen a town do a proper tree lighting before."

"Well, looks like you're in for a treat," Becket said, unable to hide his own excitement. Even though he was new to town, something about tonight was like stepping into a tradition he'd always belonged to.

As they walked toward the town square, twinkling lights cast a warm glow, and carols floated through the crisp, cold air. Becket watched Ruby—the way her eyes sparkled, reflecting every light they passed, her cheeks flushed pink from the cold. She seemed to belong here, right in the heart of Aspen Cove's winter wonderland.

"Ready for your first Aspen Cove tree lighting?" he asked, a grin spreading wide across his face.

Ruby nodded, and there was a glimmer of something more than just excitement in her eyes—something that made Becket's heart skip a beat. "You know what? I think I am."

As they walked toward the tree, Ruby reached into the basket slung over her arm, offering gingerbread cookies to people they passed. Children's faces lit up, and even a few adults couldn't resist taking one.

When they reached Maisey, the owner of the diner, Ruby held out a cookie. "Gingerbread?" she offered.

Maisey grinned, balancing a tray piled high with cookies of her own. "Well, if you insist," she said, taking one. Houdini's ears perked, and the goat tried to sneak a nibble from the edge of the tray.

"Ah, ah, ah!" Maisey swatted him away, laughing. "Not for you."

Becket shrugged apologetically. "Sorry about that. He's got a bit of a sweet tooth."

Maisey waved a dismissive hand. "Don't we all?" She nodded toward the tree, pride evident in her voice. "You know, that beauty was planted just last year. Came straight from Amanda Anderson's yard. She's an author who's writing an entire romance series about this town."

"Really?" Ruby asked, looking at the tree with new admiration. "That's so ... special."

Maisey nodded. "Aspen Cove has a way of finding its way into your heart. Just like it did with Amanda—who inherited her cabin in the woods from Bea Bennett. This town..." She looked around, her eyes sweeping over the families, the lights, the joy in the air. "It makes you want to stay. Gives you roots."

Ruby's eyes softened as she looked at Maisey, then at Becket. "Seems like Amanda and I have a lot in common."

"Maybe more than you realize," Maisey said. "Aspen Cove has a lot to offer—if you're open to seeing it."

Becket watched Ruby closely, hoping she was starting to see what Maisey meant. He could feel that sense of rightness again, that feeling like he was where he was supposed to be. And maybe Ruby was feeling it too, he thought, as she laughed at Houdini's continued attempts to steal a cookie.

Tonight was going to be special. He could feel it in the air.

CHAPTER TWENTY-ONE

Ruby gazed out at the snow-covered landscape, still marveling at the transformation Aspen Cove had undergone overnight. A fresh blanket of snow had turned the world into a glittering wonderland, so different from the city views she was accustomed to.

As she sipped her coffee, her mind wandered back to the previous evening's cookie sharing and tree lighting ceremony. The town square had been magical, with twinkling lights strung between buildings and a massive Christmas tree as the centerpiece. But what had taken her breath away was the sense of community, the way everyone had come together to celebrate.

"I still can't get over how amazing last night was," Ruby said, turning to Becket who was busy at the stove, the sizzle and aroma of bacon filling the air. "When Doc came out dressed as Santa, I couldn't believe it. For a minute there, I thought he was the real deal."

Becket's eyes lit up, crinkling at the corners in a way that made Ruby's stomach somersault. "I was surprised too.

He got into character—that beard looked like he'd been growing it all year!"

Ruby remembered how the children had gathered around Doc, their eyes wide with wonder. His belly might have been padded, but there was nothing fake about the twinkle in his eye or the heartiness of his "Ho ho ho!"

The costume had been impeccable from the rich red suit trimmed with white fur to the gleaming black boots.

"And his speech," Ruby continued, warming her hands on her mug. "It wasn't what I expected at all. No talk about shopping or gifts, just community and kindness. It was beautiful."

Becket nodded, his expression softening as he placed a plate of bacon and eggs in front of her. "Doc seems to have a way of cutting right to the heart of things."

Ruby recalled Doc's words, how he'd spoken about the true spirit of Christmas being found in acts of kindness and the bonds of community. His voice, warm and gravelly, had carried across the square, holding everyone spellbound. A longing for connection stirred within her, one she hadn't even realized she'd been missing.

As they ate their late breakfast, Ruby was reluctant to break the comfortable quiet that had settled between them. There was something so peaceful about these moments with Becket, something that made her feel grounded and content in a way she'd rarely experienced before. But the increasingly insistent bleating from outside reminded her of their responsibilities.

"Sounds like the goats are getting impatient," she said, standing up and gathering their plates. "Shall we go check on our little troublemakers?"

Becket rose to join her. "Let's see how they're faring after their big debut last night."

Walking to the garage, Ruby smiled at the memory of the goats all dressed up for the ceremony. Their bells had jingled with each step as they trotted alongside, drawing delighted laughter from everyone in the square.

"I still can't believe how well-behaved Houdini was last night," Ruby said as they entered the garage, the familiar scent of hay and animals enveloping them. "Well, aside from trying to eat those cookies."

Becket shook his head, amused. "I think Houdini was too busy basking in all the attention to cause his usual mischief last night. Though I did catch him eyeing the tinsel on the tree a few times."

As if on cue, Houdini trotted over from the corner where he'd been resting, making a beeline for Ruby. She knelt down on the concrete floor, scratching behind his ears as he nuzzled against her. His fur was soft under her fingers, and she was surprised by how attached she'd grown to these animals. Just a few weeks ago, she'd never even been close to a goat. Now, she couldn't imagine starting her day without their greetings.

"Good morning to you too, you little rascal," she cooed. Houdini bleated in response, pushing his head further into her hand. Ruby laughed, the sound echoing in the garage. "I think someone's fishing for treats."

Becket appeared beside her, a small bag of goat-friendly treats in hand. "Well, I suppose he did earn it. Just don't tell the others, or we'll never hear the end of it."

As they went about their morning routine, feeding the goats and refreshing their water, Ruby marveled at how natural it all seemed. The rhythm of this life, so foreign to her not long ago, now brought her comfort and a sense of rightness. The methodical tasks, the scent of hay they'd spread on the garage floor, the satisfied munching of the goats—it all combined to create a sense of peace she'd never known in her fast-paced city life.

She watched Becket as he walked around the garage, his movements sure and practiced. There was a grace to the way he worked, a confidence born of years of experience and genuine care for the animals. He paused near Daisy.

"How's she doing?" Ruby asked, coming to stand beside him. She peered over at Daisy, who was lying down, her sides visibly swollen with her pregnancy.

Becket ran a gentle hand along Daisy's side. "Getting close, I think. Might be any day now."

Ruby's stomach fluttered with excitement mixed with nervousness. The idea of witnessing the birth was both thrilling and a little daunting. "I hope I'm still here when it happens. I'd love to see her baby."

As soon as the words left her mouth, an unease settled in her chest. The reminder of her temporary status in Aspen Cove hung in the air between them. She noticed Becket's shoulders tense, and she wished she could take the words back. The reality of her situation—the life waiting for her back in Chicago, the decisions she had yet to make—came crashing back, shattering the peaceful bubble of the morning.

"Becket, I—" she began, but was cut off by a loud bleat from Sir Chomps-a-Lot, who had managed to get his head stuck in a feed bucket.

The tension broken, they rushed to free the goat, laughing as they worked to wiggle the bucket off his head. As Ruby held Sir Chomps-a-Lot still, Becket's hands brushed against hers, sending a shiver up her arm that had nothing to do with the garage's chill. She became acutely aware of his proximity, of the energy radiating from him, and of the way his brow furrowed in concentration as he maneuvered the bucket.

With the crisis averted, Ruby suddenly realized how close they were standing. She could see the flecks of gold in Becket's eyes, could count each of his eyelashes if she wanted to. Her heart raced, and she found herself holding her breath, though she wasn't sure what she was waiting for.

"Ruby," Becket said, his voice low and intense. "Last night, at the tree lighting ... seeing you there, with everyone ... it was right. Like you belonged."

Ruby's heart soared and sank simultaneously. She knew what he was saying, what he was asking without asking. Part of her wanted to throw caution to the wind, to tell him that yes, it did feel right, that she could see herself belonging here in Aspen Cove—with him. The thought of waking up every morning to this—to the goats, to the snow-covered fields, to Becket—was intoxicatingly appealing.

But the practical part of her, the part that had built a life and career in Chicago, held her back. The thought of her apartment, her job, her friends back in the city flashed through her mind. Could she leave all that behind for this new life that, while beautiful, was still so unfamiliar?

"Becket, I ... I don't know what to say. This place, these past few weeks ... it's all been like a dream. But I have a life back in Chicago. Responsibilities. I can't just..."

She trailed off, seeing the hope in Becket's eyes dim. It broke her heart a little, but she couldn't bring herself to make promises she wasn't sure she could keep. The weight of the decision pressed down on her, making it hard to breathe.

Becket nodded, stepping back, and the absence of his presence was immediate. "I get it. I don't want to put you on the spot. But just so you know ... this place, this town—it's already made room for you, if you want to be a part of it."

The sincerity in his voice made Ruby's chest ache. She opened her mouth to respond, though she wasn't sure what she was going to say, when a distressed bleat from Daisy's pen caught their attention.

They turned to see the pregnant goat pacing restlessly, occasionally pawing at the ground. Daisy's discomfort was evident, and concern welled up in Ruby for the animal she'd grown so fond of.

"Is she okay?" Ruby asked, concern momentarily over-riding the emotional tension of the moment.

Becket moved to Daisy's side, his practiced hands running along her swollen belly. His face showed both concentration and excitement as he examined the goat. "I think," he said, his voice full of excitement, "we might be about to welcome a new Shepherd baby."

Ruby's eyes widened, her heart rate picking up. "You mean she's in labor? Now? What do we do?"

Becket turned to her, his earlier vulnerability replaced by a calm determination. There was a steadiness to him in this moment that Ruby found incredibly reassuring. "First, we make her comfortable. Then, we wait. Nature usually takes its course, but we'll be here if she needs us." He paused, then added, "That is if you want to stay and help. I know it wasn't in your plans for today..."

Ruby didn't hesitate. Despite her uncertainties about the future, despite the weight of the decisions looming over her, she knew with absolute certainty that there was nowhere else she'd rather be right now. "Of course I'll stay. I wouldn't want to be anywhere else."

As they set about preparing for Daisy's impending

delivery, a sense of rightness settled over Ruby. The uncertainty about her future, the pull between Chicago and Aspen Cove, faded into the background.

They worked together seamlessly, Becket guiding her through the process of preparing for the birth. Ruby admired his knowledge and gentle handling of Daisy. She fetched clean towels, helped spread fresh straw, and stood by, ready to assist in any way she could.

The hours ticked by, marked by Daisy's increasing discomfort and their quiet words of encouragement. Ruby whispered soothing words to the goat, her hand stroking Daisy's side. She was surprised by how invested she was, how much she cared about this animal and the little life about to enter the world.

As Daisy's labor progressed, Ruby stood shoulder to shoulder with Becket, ready to face whatever came next—together. In that moment, surrounded by the coziness of the garage and the gentle sounds of the goats, Ruby realized that sometimes, the most unexpected detours in life could lead to the most beautiful destinations.

The day stretched ahead of them, full of promise and possibility. And as they waited for a new life to enter the world, Ruby sensed that something new was beginning for her as well. Whatever the future held, whatever decisions lay ahead, she knew that this moment, this experience, would stay with her forever.

As evening approached, Daisy surprisingly gave birth to twins—a boy and a girl. Ruby and Becket watched the newborn goats enter the world with wonder.

"We should name them," Becket said.

Ruby nodded. "I have an idea. How about Baguette for the girl?"

"Baguette," Becket repeated, chuckling. "I like it. Then let's call the boy Crouton."

"Perfect," Ruby agreed. "Baguette and Crouton."

They watched as Baguette and Crouton snuggled up to Daisy, beginning their new life together.

CHAPTER TWENTY-TWO

The late afternoon sun cast long shadows across the snow-covered yard as Becket finished checking on the goats. It had been a whirlwind few days since Daisy had given birth to twins on that eventful morning. The newest additions to their little herd were now settled in the makeshift pen Becket and Ruby had constructed in the garage, allowing them to keep a closer eye on the newborns.

Christmas Eve had arrived, and the air was filled with a sense of anticipation. As Becket made his way back to the house, he paused to take in the sight before him. Ruby's uncle's old place, once a cluttered mess, now looked warm and inviting with twinkling lights adorning the porch and a wreath hanging on the door—all put up in a flurry of activity between caring for Daisy and her kids.

Inside, the house was alive with the sounds and scents of Christmas. Ruby had found an old record player and was playing classic carols as she put the finishing touches on their hastily but lovingly arranged decorations. The scent of pine from their freshly cut tree filled the room, while faint traces of gingerbread lingered from the cookies they'd baked a few days ago for the exchange.

"Hey there, Goat Whisperer," Ruby called out as Becket stamped the snow off his boots. "Everything okay with our four-legged friends?"

Becket nodded, hanging up his coat. "All good. Daisy and the twins are settling in nicely. Who would've thought we'd be goat grandparents before Christmas?"

Ruby laughed, the sound warming Becket more than any fire could. The shared experience of helping Daisy through her delivery had brought them closer, breaking down some of the barriers that had existed between them.

As he moved further into the house, Becket was struck by how different everything looked. In just a few short days, they'd transformed the space. Gone were the piles of Uncle Peter's eclectic collections. In their place were tasteful decorations and the warm glow of candles. It was home in a way Becket had never experienced before.

"This place looks amazing, Ruby," he said, taking it all in. "You've worked some magic here."

Ruby beamed, her cheeks flushing at the compliment. "Thanks. I found some of Uncle Peter's old decorations in the attic. It just seemed right to use them, you know?"

Becket nodded, understanding. He'd grown fond of the old house, just as he'd grown fond of the woman standing before him.

As they prepared a simple Christmas Eve dinner, Becket found himself drawn to Ruby's every movement. The way she hummed along to the carols, her focused expression while chopping vegetables—it all captivated him. Her presence filled the room, making everything feel just right.

It wasn't until they were sitting down to eat that the

realization hit him like a ton of bricks. Gifts. They hadn't gotten gifts for each other.

Becket froze, his fork halfway to his mouth. How could he have forgotten something so important? He glanced at Ruby, who was happily eating her meal. She didn't seem to have realized the oversight.

"Hey, uh, I just remembered," Becket said, trying to keep his voice casual, "I need to run into town for a bit. Forgot to pick up ... cranberry sauce. For tomorrow's dinner."

Ruby looked up, her brow furrowed. "Cranberry sauce? I didn't know we were having turkey."

"Oh, well, you know," Becket fumbled, "it's good with other things too. Ham. Or ... goat."

Ruby raised an eyebrow but didn't question him further. "Alright. If you're sure. Don't be too long, though. It's getting dark."

Becket nodded, already planning his gift-hunting strategy as he grabbed his coat and headed out the door.

The streets of Aspen Cove were quieter than usual, most folks already settled in for their Christmas Eve celebrations. A moment of panic seized Becket. What could he possibly get for Ruby that would convey how much she'd come to mean to him in such a short time? He didn't have much money to spend, but he'd use every cent he had left in his account to make her happy.

He ducked into the Corner Store, hoping for inspiration. As he wandered the aisles, his mind raced. What did Ruby like? What would make her eyes light up with that little spark he'd grown to love?

"Looking for something special, son?"

Becket turned to find Doc standing behind him grinning.

"Doc! I, uh ... yeah. I'm trying to find a gift for Ruby."

Doc's smile widened. "Ah, left it to the last minute, did you? Well, let me tell you something about gift-giving. It's not about how much you spend or how fancy it is. It's about showing you've been paying attention."

Becket nodded, considering Doc's words. Paying attention... Suddenly, an idea began to form.

"Thanks, Doc," he said, clapping the older man on the shoulder. "I think I know just what to do."

With renewed purpose, Becket set about gathering the items he needed. By the time he left the store, his arms were full of bags and his heart was light with anticipation.

As he walked home, the snow crunching softly under his boots, Becket found himself wondering if Ruby had gotten him a gift. He shook his head. It didn't matter—she was the gift, and that was more than enough.

When he returned, the house was bathed in the soft glow of candlelight. Ruby was curled up on the couch, a mug of hot cocoa in her hands, her gaze fixed on the twinkling lights of the Christmas tree.

"You're back," she said, smiling up at him. "Did you get your cranberry sauce?"

Becket nodded, setting his bags down out of sight. "Yep, all set for tomorrow."

He joined Ruby on the couch, and they sat in comfortable silence, listening to the crackle of the fire and the soft strains of "Silent Night" playing on the record player.

"You know," Ruby said after a while, "I never thought I'd be spending Christmas like this. In a small town, in my uncle's old house, with..." She trailed off, her cheeks flushing.

"With a goat farmer?" Becket supplied, grinning.

Ruby laughed, the sound warming Becket more than

any fire could. "Yeah, with a goat farmer. But I wouldn't change it for anything."

Becket's heart swelled at her words. He wanted to tell her everything—how she'd changed his life in just a few short weeks. But the moment wasn't quite right. Instead, he simply said, "Me neither, Ruby. Me neither."

As the night wore on, they shared stories of past Christmases, laughing at childhood memories and family traditions. Becket's thoughts drifted to future holidays, envisioning new traditions they might create together here in Aspen Cove. It was late when they decided to turn in for the night. As they stood to head to their room, an urge surged through Becket to hold on to this moment just a little longer.

"Ruby," he said, his voice soft, "I'm glad you're here. That we're here, together."

Ruby's eyes shined in the low light. "So am I, Becket. Merry Christmas."

"Merry Christmas, Ruby."

CHAPTER TWENTY-THREE

Ruby stood by the Christmas tree, absently adjusting an ornament as the late morning sun streamed through the windows of Uncle Peter's old house. Her mind wandered to the events of the previous night, replaying every touch, every kiss, every word. Becket had made love to her with such tenderness, such intensity—as if it might be the last time. The thought sent a shiver down her spine, equal parts thrilling and unsettling.

She closed her eyes, remembering the feel of Becket's calloused hands on her skin, the gentle brush of his breath against her neck. He'd held her like she was precious, something to be cherished and protected. It had been passionate, yes, but also tinged with a desperation that Ruby couldn't quite shake.

Was he planning on leaving? The question nagged at her. Becket had only ever been meant to be temporary help, a kind stranger lending a hand with Uncle Peter's house. When he arrived, the goats had been an unexpected addition, but somewhere along the way, Becket had become so much more. He'd become the first person she thought of in the morning and the last person she wanted to see at night. He'd become ... everything.

The back door opened, snapping Ruby out of her reverie. She turned to see Becket stamping snow off his boots, his cheeks flushed from the cold. Her heart did a little flip at the sight of him, even as anxiety gnawed at her stomach.

"How are they doing?" Ruby asked, trying to keep her voice casual despite the tumult of emotions inside her.

Becket's eyes met hers, his gaze filled with tenderness. "They're good. Daisy and the kids are settling in nicely. Houdini tried to eat my shoelaces, so everything's normal there."

Ruby laughed, the sound easing some of the tension that had been building since they'd woken up in each other's arms. They hadn't talked about the deepening of their relationship, both seemingly afraid to disrupt the delicate balance of their growing intimacy.

"I made some fresh coffee," Ruby said, gesturing towards the kitchen. "Thought we might need it before ... well, before we open gifts."

Becket nodded. "Sounds perfect."

As they moved to the kitchen, Ruby studied Becket's profile. How had this man, who'd started as a stranger, become so essential to her in such a short time? The way he moved with quiet confidence, the gentle strength in his hands as he poured their coffee—it all spoke to a depth of character that drew her in.

They sat at the small table, their eyes meeting over the rims of their mugs. The air between them was charged, filled with unspoken words and new possibilities. Ruby wanted to ask him about his plans, about whether he intended to stay in Aspen Cove or if last night had been a beautiful goodbye. But the words stuck in her throat, fear of the answer holding her back.

"So," Becket began, his voice a little rough. "Last night was..."

"Yeah," Ruby agreed, her cheeks warming. "It was."

They just looked at each other, both searching for the right words. Becket reached across the table, taking Ruby's hand in his.

"I don't regret it," he said, his thumb tracing small circles on her palm. "Not for a second. But I need you to know that I don't expect anything. If you're still planning to go back to Chicago..."

Ruby's heart constricted. Here he was, giving her an out, when what she really wanted was to understand where they stood. She squeezed his hand. "I don't regret it either," she said. "And as for Chicago ... that feels like another life. I don't know what the future holds, but right now, I'm here. And I'm happy."

Becket let out a small breath. "I'm happy you're here too."

They finished their coffee in comfortable silence, hands still linked across the table. As they stood to rinse their mugs, Becket's arm brushed against Ruby's, sending a jolt of awareness through her. She turned to face him, acutely aware of how close they were standing.

For a heartbeat, it seemed like Becket might kiss her. Ruby's breath caught in her throat, torn between wanting him to close the distance and needing to understand where they stood. But then the moment passed, and he stepped back.

"Should we ... open presents?" he asked, a hint of nervousness in his voice.

Ruby nodded, both disappointed and relieved. "Yes, let's do that."

As they moved to the living room where the gifts waited under the tree, Ruby's mind raced. What did Becket's gift mean in light of last night? Was it a parting gift or a promise of more to come? And what would her own gift reveal about her feelings, her hopes for the future?

With trembling hands, she reached for the messily wrapped package Becket handed her, her heart pounding with anticipation and a touch of fear. Whatever was inside this package, she knew it had the power to change everything.

Ruby's fingers trembled as she began to unwrap Becket's gift. The paper crinkled, the sound unnaturally loud in the quiet room. As she peeled back the last of the wrapping, she revealed a large mason jar filled with folded pieces of colorful paper, accompanied by a basket brimming with local treats.

"It's a memory jar," Becket explained, his voice soft and a touch nervous. "I wrote down all the moments we've shared here in Aspen Cove. And the basket ... well, I thought you might like a taste of the town to take with you. Or ... to enjoy here. If you want."

Tears pricked at Ruby's eyes as she lifted the jar, seeing glimpses of Becket's handwriting on the folded papers inside. She opened one at random, reading aloud, "The way you laughed when Houdini stole your scarf."

The memory flooded back, vivid and warm. It had been a crisp afternoon, not long after she'd arrived in Aspen Cove. Becket had been showing her how to feed the goats, and she'd been so focused on not dropping the feed bucket that she hadn't noticed Houdini sneaking up behind her. The goat had snagged her scarf right off her neck, prancing away with his prize. She'd been startled at first, but Becket's laughter had been infectious, and soon they were both doubled over, watching Houdini parade around the garage with the scarf trailing behind him like a royal train.

Ruby looked up at Becket, her heart full. "This is perfect, Becket. Thank you."

She reached into the jar again, pulling out another slip of paper. "The look on your face when you tasted Maisey's apple pie for the first time."

Another memory washed over her. They'd stopped at the diner after a long day of sorting through Uncle Peter's belongings. Ruby had been feeling overwhelmed and home-sick, but one bite of that pie had transported her. The rich spices, the perfect balance of tart and sweet—it had felt like home in a way she couldn't explain. She remembered looking up to find Becket was watching her, a look in his eyes that made her heart skip a beat.

"I can't believe you remembered all these moments," Ruby said, her voice thick with emotion.

Becket moved closer, his hand coming to rest on her shoulder. "I remember everything about our time together, Ruby. Every smile, every laugh ... every moment I've fallen a little more in love with you."

Ruby's breath caught in her throat. Hearing him say it so openly still felt like a milestone, even though they had both hinted at it before. Now, the word "love" hung between them, full of promise and possibility.

She turned to the basket next, exploring its contents. There was a jar of local honey, a package of Katie's famous brownies, a bag of coffee from the Corner Store, and various other treats that represented the flavors of Aspen Cove. Each item sparked another memory—lazy mornings sharing coffee, and late-night snacks as they pored over Uncle Peter's papers.

"Becket, this is…" Ruby trailed off, overwhelmed by the thoughtfulness of the gift and the emotions it stirred.

"Too much?" Becket asked, a hint of worry in his voice.

Ruby shook her head emphatically. "No, it's perfect. It's just … last night, when we were together, it was like…"

"Like what?" Becket prompted when she hesitated.

Ruby took a deep breath. "Like you were saying good-bye. Like it might be the last time. And now this gift… Are you planning on leaving, Becket?"

Becket's eyes widened in surprise. "Leaving? Ruby, no. I thought … I thought you might be the one leaving. Going back to Chicago. That's why I wanted you to have these memories, these tastes of Aspen Cove. So, you'd have a piece of this place—a piece of us—wherever you went."

Relief flooded through Ruby, followed by a wave of affection for this man who had so thoroughly captured her heart. "Oh, Becket," she said, reaching out to cup his cheek. "I don't want to leave. I don't think I could, even if I tried. This place, these people … you. It all feels like home now."

Becket leaned into her touch, his eyes shining with emotion. "You have no idea how happy I am to hear that."

They stayed like that, savoring the newfound certainty between them. Then Ruby remembered her own gift. "Oh! You still need to open yours."

She reached for the neatly wrapped package under the tree, nerves fluttering as she wondered how her gift would compare to Becket's thoughtful offering. "It's not as elaborate as yours, but I hope you'll like it."

Becket took the package, unwrapping it to reveal a

leather-bound notebook. He opened it, his eyebrows rising in surprise as he flipped through the pages.

"It's a business plan," Ruby explained. "For expanding our little yard-based goat farm. I've been doing some research, and I think there's real potential here—artisanal goat cheese, soap made from goat milk, even goat yoga classes. I know it might seem presumptuous, but I thought ... well, I thought maybe we could build something together. Here in Aspen Cove."

Becket looked up from the notebook, his eyes shining. "Ruby, this is ... it's incredible. You've put so much thought into this. But are you sure? This would mean staying here, changing your whole life."

Ruby nodded, feeling more certain than she had about anything in a long time. "I'm sure. Last night, being with you ... it felt right, Becket. Like everything in my life had been leading me here, to you, to this place. I want to see where this can go. I want to build a life here, with you."

Becket set the notebook aside, then pulled Ruby into his arms. "I love you," he said. "I think I've loved you since the day you let me and the goats camp in your yard ... or maybe it was when you brought me those old crackers and rancid peanut butter for a meal."

Ruby laughed, wrapping her arms around him. "I love you too. Even if you do smell like goats most of the time."

They stayed in each other's arms for a long moment, the twinkling lights of the Christmas tree casting a warm glow over them. Eventually, Becket pulled back. "Speaking of goats, it's a good idea to check on Daisy and the kids. Make sure they're not feeling neglected on their first Christmas."

Ruby nodded, smiling. "Lead the way, Goat Whisperer."

Hand in hand, they strolled to the garage. The air was

crisp and cold, their breath forming small clouds in the fading light. Inside, warmth greeted them, along with the gentle rustling and soft bleats.

Daisy was curled up in her corner, her two kids nestled against her side. Houdini and Sir Chomps-a-Lot were huddled together nearby, looking for all the world like they were plotting their next coup.

"Merry Christmas, you troublemakers," Becket said fondly, reaching out to scratch behind Houdini's ears.

As they tended to the goats, refilling water and providing some holiday treats, Ruby was struck by how natural it all seemed. The rhythm of this life, once so foreign to her, now seemed like second nature. She watched Becket move around the garage with effortless familiarity, as if he could do it in his sleep. There was something comforting in his ease, and it gave her a quiet surge of love and certainty.

This was where she belonged. Here in Aspen Cove, with Becket, building a life surrounded by the close-knit community and the unconditional love of a herd of trouble-making goats.

She looked back at the scene—the contented goats, the warm glow of the single bulb hanging from the ceiling, Becket giving Daisy one last pat—and knew she'd made the right choice.

"What are you thinking?" Becket asked, coming to stand beside her.

Ruby leaned into him, resting her head on his shoulder. "I'm thinking that this is the best Christmas I've ever had. And I can't wait to see what the new year brings."

Becket pressed a kiss to the top of her head. "Whatever it brings, we'll face it together. You, me, and a bunch of goats."

Ruby laughed, the sound echoing in the crisp winter air. As they walked back to the house, hand in hand, a sense of peace settled over her. The future stretched out before them, full of possibility and promise. And Ruby knew, with absolute certainty, that the best was yet to come.

Three months later

Becket paused his work with the tiller, straightening to stretch his back and wipe the sweat from his brow. The warm spring sun beat down on him, a welcome change from the harsh winter they'd just endured. As he looked out over the field, memories of the past few months flooded his mind.

The winter had passed in a whirlwind of cozy moments and careful planning. He and Ruby had huddled together in the old house, now their shared home, dreaming up their future. With Ruby's business acumen and his farming experience, they'd crafted a plan to transform the home-based goat farm into a thriving artisanal cheese business.

Nights were spent poring over books on cheese-making and animal husbandry, while days were filled with caring for their growing herd and preparing for the spring. Through it all, their love had deepened, rooted in shared dreams and the simple joys of building a life together.

Now, as the first real days of spring had arrived, they stood ready to embark on their new adventure, armed with determination, a solid plan, and a herd of goats eager to play their part.

Becket's gaze drifted across the yard to where Ruby was marking out plots for their herb garden. The sight of her, so at home here, never failed to make his heart swell with affection.

"How's it coming, darlin'?" he called out.

Ruby straightened, pushing a stray lock of hair from her face, leaving a smudge of dirt on her cheek. "Almost done! This is going to be perfect for the chevre seasonings."

Becket grinned, still amazed at how Ruby had taken to this life. Her enthusiasm was infectious, and her creativity seemed boundless. Just last week, she'd come up with the perfect name for their new venture: "Goat Town Creamery: Where Mischief Meets Flavor."

Their improvements had come courtesy of an unexpected discovery in Uncle Peter's attic where she found an entire collection of vintage action figures—G.I. Joes, Transformers, even a few rare Star Wars toys—all still in their original packaging.

Ruby had nearly doubled over with laughter when they realized how much the toys were worth. "I guess Uncle Peter was onto something after all," she'd said with a grin. The auction had brought in more than enough to build the new goat barn and fund their expansions.

Becket's eyes crinkled with amusement as he shook his head. "Are you up for a milking lesson?"

Ruby's eyes lit up with excitement. "Absolutely! Let me just finish this last row."

A few minutes later, they were in the barn, the sweet smell of hay and the soft sounds of the goats creating a peaceful atmosphere. Becket led Ruby to Daisy's stall, the gentle girl watching them with curious eyes.

"Alright," Becket said, positioning the stool. "The key is to be gentle but firm. You want to create a seal with your thumb and forefinger, then squeeze with the rest of your hand."

Ruby nodded, her face a mask of concentration as she began to milk Daisy. Her first attempts were a bit clumsy, but soon she found her rhythm, streams of milk hitting the pail with a satisfying ping.

"I'm doing it!" she exclaimed, looking up at Becket with a proud grin.

Becket's heart swelled with affection. "You're a natural," he said, leaning down to press a kiss to the top of her head.

As Ruby finished milking Daisy, Becket heard a commotion from the other end of the barn. He turned to see Houdini, true to his name, attempting to squeeze through a gap between the stall boards.

"Oh no, you don't," Becket said, rushing over to guide the goat back into his stall. "I swear, Houdini, you're more trouble than all the others combined."

Ruby laughed, coming over to scratch behind Houdini's ears. "But he's so adorable, aren't you, you little escape artist?" The goat bleated, leaning into her touch.

Becket shook his head, amused. "Don't encourage him. Next thing you know, we'll find him in the kitchen, eating our cheese supplies."

As if understanding the conversation, Sir Chomps-a-Lot let out a loud sound from his stall. Ruby giggled. "I think someone's feeling left out."

They made their rounds, checking on each goat. Daisy's kids were growing rapidly; Sir Chomps-a-Lot was, as always, on the lookout for food; gentle Buttercup grazed calmly; and, of course, there was Houdini, the troublemaker. Then there were Butterscotch, Pickles, Biscuit, and Nugget—less trouble but full of personality. Becket loved watching Ruby with them, her initial city-girl hesitation long gone.

After ensuring all the goats were fed and comfortable, they headed to the cheese-making room. Becket watched as Ruby added culture to the fresh milk, her movements precise and confident.

"You know," he said, wrapping his arms around her waist from behind, "I never thought I'd find someone who'd be excited about making goat cheese with me."

Ruby leaned back into his embrace. "And I never thought I'd fall in love with a goat farmer and leave city life behind. Funny how things work out, isn't it?"

As they worked side by side, stirring curds and checking temperatures, a knock at the barn door surprised them.

"Hello? Anybody home?" called a familiar voice.

Becket opened the door to find Maisey, holding a basket.

"Maisey! What brings you out here?"

The older woman stepped forward. "Just thought I'd bring you two some lunch. Figured you'd be too busy to cook with all this exciting new business starting up."

Ruby wiped her hands on her apron, coming to greet Maisey. "That's so thoughtful of you! Please, come in and see what we've been working on."

As Maisey entered, her eyes widened, taking in the setup. "Well, would you look at that! You two have been busy little bees, haven't you?"

"We're trying our best," Becket said. "Maisey, we were hoping to talk to you about featuring some of our cheeses at the diner once we're up and running."

Maisey's face lit up. "Oh, I'd love that! Nothing better

than locally sourced products. And coming from you two? It's bound to be delicious."

As they chatted, sharing Maisey's homemade sandwiches and discussing potential cheese flavors for the diner, a sense of belonging settled over Becket that had nothing to do with the spring sunshine. This was community; this was home.

Their lunch was interrupted by a car pulling up. Through the barn door, Becket saw Doc's old pickup truck coming to a stop.

"Looks like news travels fast in Aspen Cove," Ruby said.

Doc entered the barn, his eyes twinkling with curiosity. "Well, well, what do we have here? Maisey said you two were starting up a cheese business, but I had to see it for myself."

Becket led the older man to a converted shed just off the barn, their small but efficient cheese-making setup. Shelves lined the walls, stocked with supplies, and a stainless-steel workbench occupied the center. As they walked through, Becket explained their plans, detailing each part of the process. Doc nodded approvingly, asking insightful questions about the equipment, the cheese-making process, and the care of the goats.

"You know," Doc said, stroking his beard thoughtfully, "my arthritis has been acting up something fierce lately. I've heard goat milk soap can be good for that. Any plans to branch out into that area?"

Ruby and Becket exchanged looks. "We've talked about that," Ruby said. "It's definitely on our list."

As the afternoon wore on, more townspeople dropped by, each bringing well-wishes, advice, and often, offers of help. Mrs. Brown promised to knit some cozy sweaters for the baby goats. Katie suggested featuring Goat Town

Creamery products in her shop's spring menu. Even Sheriff Cooper stopped by, jokingly asking if they needed any security measures to keep Houdini in check.

By the time the last visitor left, the sun was starting to set. Becket and Ruby stood in the doorway of the barn, looking out over their property, now bathed in the golden light of dusk.

"I can't believe how supportive everyone is," Ruby said, leaning into Becket's side.

Becket wrapped an arm around her shoulders, a note of wonder in his voice. "Yeah, I didn't expect this, either. But I guess that's Aspen Cove for you. They know how to make you feel like family."

They were about to head inside when a soft bleat caught their attention. Turning, they saw Houdini had managed to open his stall door and was trotting towards them.

"Oh, for heaven's sake," Becket groaned, amusement evident in his voice. "Come on, you troublemaker. Back to bed."

As they herded Houdini back to his stall, making sure to secure the latch this time, a deep sense of satisfaction washed over Becket. This was his life now—caring for goats, making cheese, and building a future with the woman he loved, all while surrounded by the support of a close-knit community.

Later that evening, as they sat on the porch watching the stars come out, Ruby pulled out her sketchpad. "I've been working on some logo designs," she said, flipping to a page filled with sketches. "What do you think about this one?"

Becket leaned in, examining the playful design of a grinning goat wearing a chef's hat. "It's perfect," he said, his voice filled with admiration. "Captures the spirit of the place, that's for sure."

Ruby beamed, already reaching for her laptop. "Great! I'll finalize it and start working on the website and some ad concepts."

As Ruby dove into her design work, Becket marveled at how seamlessly their skills complemented each other. His practical farming knowledge and her business and creative expertise were proving to be a powerful combination.

"You know," he said, taking her hand in his, "I think we might just make this crazy dream work."

Ruby squeezed his hand, her eyes shining with love and determination. "I know we will. Together, we can handle anything—even a herd of goats and a town full of eager taste-testers."

As if in agreement, a chorus of bleats rose from the barn. Their journey was just beginning, but with love, hard work, and a touch of goat-inspired mischief, Becket knew that Goat Town Creamery was bound for success.

He thought back to that first day he met Ruby. She was determined to sell the place and leave it all behind. She hadn't planned to stay, just wanted to clean up the yard, put it on the market, and be done with it. But a storm, and a bunch of goats, had other plans. Now, she was as much a part of this land as the goats or the pine trees. And as for himself, Becket had found a home and a purpose he'd never dreamed possible.

Spring had brought new life to the yard, but more than that, it had brought the promise of a future filled with love, laughter, plenty of goat cheese, and a community that was like family. And Becket wouldn't have it any other way.

OTHER BOOKS BY KELLY COLLINS

Dive into heartwarming romance, unforgettable love stories, and second chances. Explore all of Kelly Collins' series and find your next favorite happily-ever-after!

Recipes for Love

A Taste of Temptation

A Pinch of Passion

A Dash of Desire

A Cup of Compassion

A Dollop of Delight

A Layer of Love

Recipe for Love Collection 1-3

Recipe for Love Collection 4-6

The Second Chance Series

Set Free

Set Aside

Set in Stone

Set Up

Set on You

The Second Chance Series Box Set

A Pure Decadence Series

Yours to Have

Yours to Conquer

GET A FREE BOOK.

Go to www.authorkellycollins.com

ABOUT THE AUTHOR

International bestselling author of over 50 novels, Kelly Collins crafts stories that keep love alive. With a heart full of romance and a vivid imagination, she blends real-life events into captivating tales that contemporary romance, new adult, and romantic suspense fans will fall for over and over again.

For More Information
www.authorkellycollins.com
kelly@authorkellycollins.com